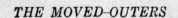

THE MOVED-OUTERS

THE
MOVED
OUTERS

FLORENCE CRANNELL MEANS

ILLUSTRATED BY HELEN BLAIR

HOUGHTON MIFFLIN COMPANY

BOSTON

The Riverside Press
CAMBRIDGE · MASSACHUSETTS
PRINTED IN THE U.S.A.

CONTENTS

Books by

FLORENCE CRANNELL MEANS

PENNY FOR LUCK

A BOWLFUL OF STARS

A CANDLE IN THE MIST

RANCH AND RING

DUSKY DAY

TANGLED WATERS

THE SINGING WOOD

SHUTTERED WINDOWS

ADELLA MARY IN OLD NEW MEXICO

AT THE END OF NOWHERE

WHISPERING GIRL

SHADOW OVER WIDE RUIN

TERESITA OF THE VALLEY

THE MOVED-OUTERS

THE MOVED–OUTERS

1

BRIGHT WEEKEND

Afterward, the weekend seemed enchanted. If it held any dull moments, they were lost in the shine of its happiness.

Yet this Friday afternoon was no different from countless others in Sue Ohara's eighteen years. She and Emily Andrews walked home from high school just as they had walked home from kindergarten: together. The same California sun shone warm on their tanned faces and bare knees, the same soft breeze played with the hair that hung at their shoulders, Emily's red hair cut and curled under to match Sue's black.

Not till afterward did Sue dream how good it was simply to walk home with her best friend in the sunshine. Now she took it for granted. 'And one of the things you learn when you grow up,' she told herself later, 'is never to take happiness for granted.'

She did not guess how good it was to scud up her own front walk and the steps of her own vine-hung porch with Emily, and push open the door and call 'Mom!' the minute her head was inside. Same door, same call, ever since kindergarten days. Same initials on the jamb where Kim had tried out his first jack-knife — Kim had been sent to bed without his supper. Same initials, S.O., with a heart around them, scratched in the cement walk. Same little ache as Sue thought of the boy who had scratched them there years ago, when they were both children.

'Hi, Mom!' she called. 'Hi-yah, Skip!'

Same scramble of paws, nails clicking on glossy wood; same Skippy capering around her, head cocked, ears flap-

ping, stubby tail ecstatic. The fox terrier had been hers
and Kim's since she was four and her brother three. The
years should have quieted him, but he still greeted his
family as if each return was a blessing despaired of. He
was a bother. His white hairs were woven firmly into the
Ohara clothing and lay in wait on the Ohara automobile
seats. He had to be walked. He had to be given other
special attentions because of his age. Yet, afterward, Sue
would look back upon Skippy's welcome longingly. To be
loved with such abandon!

And the same mother answering in a cool voice that re-
proved Sue's plunging eagerness even while she loved it.
Prim little Mother! Sue wished her voice were as soft as
that. Would her face ever be as smoothly finished? And
when she was an old woman of forty-five would her mouth
shape itself so fascinatingly when she talked?

'Have you had a pleasant day?' Mrs. Ohara asked, her
upper lip, fine as a scarlet thread, drawing down quaintly
to meet the full lower lip.

Impetuously Sue kissed the mouth, hugged the slim
body as Emily would have hugged her mother's, and then
giggled when Mrs. Ohara turned a cool cheek.

'Em,' Sue said, pinching her mother's unresponsive
shoulder, 'take a look at our Christmas stuff.'

Emily prowled around dining table and buffet. They
were crowded with gifts and stacks of gay tissue paper;
piled with finished parcels. 'Good land!' she protested.
'I haven't even bought mine. It's only the fifth of December, isn't it? "Sixteen more shopping days ——"'

'But think how horrible if Amy and Tad had to go without their Christmas! Look at the yummy cookies, Em.'

Sue tilted up a box cover and estimated her chances of
abstracting one of the nutty disks. Mrs. Ohara quietly
removed her daughter's hand and closed the box.

'Well, I wouldn't mind so much if old Tad were going to eat them all,' Sue said mournfully. 'But he'll be lucky if he gets a quarter of them. The Army seems to make men ravenous.'

'I know,' said Emily. 'Like Dick. He says every man in his barracks can smell Mother's packages in the mail. He says in two minutes flat he's holding an empty box.'

'Soldiers aren't the only folks that get hungry,' Sue said, clutching the middle of her blue sweater.

'There are a few cookies left,' Mrs. Ohara admitted. 'You'd better get your share before Kim comes.'

With a swirl of plaid skirts, Sue and Emily pushed open the swinging door. The kitchen stood expectant in the afternoon sun. Not a spoon was out of place, not a cupboard door ajar, yet the room did not forbid. It invited. Its crisp curtains lifted in the breeze. Its spice-sugar-coffee smell was as warm as its porcelain and chromium were cool. On a shelf above the sink a fat yellow cooky jar made snug promises.

Gloatingly Sue snatched off the lid. The girls bolted a cooky each, counted what were left, took four more, and shoved the jar reluctantly back in place.

In the dining room, Skippy darted between Sue's feet, watching her hands and mouth, and she broke off a fragment and held it in air. The dog came up on his hind legs and gyrated below the morsel, front paws drooping, tense throat emitting small grumbles and sighs. The cooky dropped and he snapped and gulped at the same instant.

'Mrs. Ohara, these are surely swell,' Emily said devoutly. 'Would you mind if I took the recipe?'

'Last *Journal*,' Sue said thickly. 'No, Skip, no! Can't I take a bite without your yearning at me?'

Emily said: 'Maybe you'd help me make some tonight, Sue? I'll get nuts on the way home, and do my practicing before dinner ——' Talking over her shoulder, she turned to rush out the hall door and crashed head-on into Kim, who was rushing in.

'Gollies, girl!' he exclaimed, hopping on one foot while he held the door open for her. 'Gollies, folks have to be careful of me. I might break.'

Emily ran giggling through the hall, and Kim seized his sister by the arm and sniffed noisily. 'What you been eating?' he demanded, as she swallowed her last mouthful and twisted to free herself. 'Show papa!'

Mrs. Ohara slanted a glance at them from the square of gold brocade paper she was cutting. 'Wild children,' she murmured. 'Like ten-year-olds. When I was eighteen —— My son, there are cookies in the kitchen. Don't be uncouth.'

The two raced for the cooky jar and returned somewhat pacified.

'The debate?' Mrs. Ohara inquired. 'How did it come out?'

'Mom, you should have heard him.' Sue licked the crumbs from her lips and swept her hair dramatically backward. '"Resolved that a democracy CAN be efficient!"' she declaimed. 'John Adams wasn't half bad. He had the negative. He brought up the kingdom of Denmark, how much more efficient it is, and scientific and all that; and how far Japan's literacy is above ours; and I thought Kim was a goner. But, gosh, no, Kim comes back at him with New Zealand and a bunch of other democracies and bowls them over.'

Perched on the edge of the table, Kim munched cookies and tossed an occasional bite to Skippy. His intense face was still flushed from the wordy battle of the debate, and Sue observed him indulgently. He was lean and tall, a head taller than she, though a year younger. She knew that she stood more solidly on the earth than he, in spirit as well as body, and she had looked after him and tried vigorously to make him over, from the day when he took his first step alone. Then his uncertain spread legs, wildly triumphant, had walked him off the top of the long front stairs, and it had been weeks before he got courage to try again.

Sue was always seesawing from puzzled disapproval of her brother to admiring tenderness and back. That afternoon his fiery patriotism had both impressed and embarrassed her. She could see him on the platform now, standing tall and rangy, a lock of hair flopping into his eyes, and his gestures awkward but convincing.

'When John got to howling about patriotism,' Sue went on with a reminiscent chuckle, 'as if it had gone out of style along with beards and bustles, Kim certainly got hot under the collar, Mom. He quoted the Bible and Lincoln and poetry and the encyclopedia. Still and all, he wasn't bad.'

Kim scowled. 'John and his gang act so darned superior. Of course nobody with a lick of sense would deny that stuff about working for the whole world instead of just a narrow selfish patriotism. But I think the guy was darn right when he said, "Internationalism begins at home." I suppose John would go off and leave his own country to the rotten politicians while he tried to raise economic standards in Timbuktu.'

Mrs. Ohara lifted delicate brows. 'I suppose it isn't worth while telling your mother whether Kim won or lost.'

Sue snorted. 'Of course he won. When he finished with chunks of the *Gettysburg Address*, it was all over but the shouting.'

Even Sue had glowed, and straightened in her seat with chills mounting her spine, when Kim repeated the mighty phrases: 'Conceived in liberty and dedicated to the proposition that all men are created equal ——'

But now she shrugged. 'I'm as keen for America as you are, Kim,' she said discontentedly. 'All the same, I can see that we're wasteful. And soft. And nobody can deny that there's race discrimination. Oh, well, I'm glad you won your old debate. It ought to help you get your scholarship.'

Scholarship. The word was a bell bringing the three Oharas to attention.

'If you don't get scholarships ——'

'Then no college,' Sue finished her mother's sentence. 'Anyway not till we can earn it ourselves.'

Mrs. Ohara tied a bow and patted it. 'It doesn't seem fair, after we sent the other two. But Tad's swimming helped with his expenses, and when your father let Amy go East we never dreamed how much more it would cost. And then two hospital bills in two years ——'

'And dollars don't grow on bushes. Not even on Dad's bushes,' Sue assented quickly, to get it said before her mother could. Mr. Ohara owned a nursery and florist shop in the small California town.

'Sis ought to go,' said Kim, shaking his head at Skippy and ending the argument by stuffing the cooky into his own mouth. 'After all, she's older,' he mumbled.

'Smarty,' she snapped, 'I only stayed behind to keep you straight.'

'I don't know what folks see in her,' he grumbled to his mother, 'but I have to admit she has most of them fooled. If scholarships went by popular vote, that little vixen would get a full four-year one easy.'

Sue gave concession for concession. 'If it was just grades that counted, you'd be way ahead of me. And you're popular enough, too.'

His popularity had often puzzled her. Old chip-on-the-shoulder, starry-eyed Kim ——

Mrs. Ohara twitched a bow here, patted a fold there, always effectively, though her attention was on her children. 'Then if you are both so popular, and so bright —'

'Oh, there's always someone to think we're getting more than our share,' Sue said soberly. 'With Kim winning the Sutter Medal, and being Cosmo Prexy and class treasurer ——'

'And this kid's got an office in every blame organization in school. You can just hear them buzzing about it: "Sue Ohara, Senior Secretary; Sue Ohara, Honor Society; Sue Ohara, Girls' Glee Club. Too much Ohara, buzz, buzz."'

'But your classmates seem so fair.'

'Gosh, it isn't the kids. The kids are fine.'

'Now is your good time,' Mrs. Ohara said. 'There's a saying that goes, "You're eating your white bread now." You ought to know you are.'

'I always did like brown bread better,' Sue muttered resentfully.

Her mother continued: 'Make the most of this while you have it, children. It was just so with your father and me, too. Through high school — those were our fine years, when we seemed like the rest.'

'And on through college, Mom,' Sue cried urgently. 'My grief, look at Amy, spending Christmas with Pat Van Loan. There isn't an older, swankier family in New York. Oh, I know these years have been swell, but the next ones! Four glorious years!' She clasped herself with both arms and crowed.

'You're doggone sure,' Kim said moodily.

'Sure I'm sure. Why shouldn't I be?' The light-hearted gaiety of campus life spilled through Sue's mind like bright souvenirs in a Memory Book.

Kim still brooded. 'I read about a guy,' he said, 'deformed — hunchback, maybe, or dwarf — but a kind of genius. It wasn't bad while he was in school. His pals acted as if he were normal. No, as if he were extra special and rare. But when he went out of college into real life — gosh, what a jolt. Sis, we've got to be braced for a jolt.'

Sue's face had clouded, too. 'But not yet, Kim,' she said. 'First come the glorious years.'

'I hope,' Kim answered.

After college, what? Well, that was the shadow. Everyone has a shadow; everyone with substance, amounting to anything. And your shadow is as much a part of you as the shape of your eyes and the color of your hair.

2

EVERYONE HAS A SHADOW

Against the fun of the weekend, the Ohara shadow thinned almost to nothing.

Friday, December 5, 1941, went its way, as bright as if life had no darkness, as secure as if it held no dynamite in its basement, with a spark inching along the fuse.

On Saturday Sue woke in her narrow Colonial bed and lay stretching and yawning, half-hearing the furious splash down the hall where her brother snorted and fought the bath water, her mother's light steps below. Half-hearing the papery clatter of palm leaves, the sweet dissonances of mockingbirds with Skippy barking at them. Half-sensing California odors and breakfast odors: roses and pepper trees, bacon and coffee.

Breakfast over, Father went to the shop, Kim cut the

lawn, adding grass fragrance to the scented air, Sue and Mother flew through routine tasks and attacked the Christmas packing.

'Won't Amy be a love in that raspberry sweater and skirt?' Sue thought aloud, putting in a last sumptuous parcel. 'She's so much more becoming to sweaters than I am. I suppose I eat too many cookies.'

'Now the green stuff your father brought from the nursery,' Mrs. Ohara said.

Sue carried in from the back porch the fragrant branches of pine, the holly and mistletoe, the heather with purple bells. Before laying them in place, Mother ticked off the presents, to be sure none had hidden themselves on closet shelf or in dresser drawer. In one box, fudge, cookies, pajamas, smart crêpe ones made by Mother. From Sue and Kim a flat copper necklace and bracelet, done in their school craft classes. The raspberry and gray plaid skirt and the matching sweater. In the other box, a sturdy O.D. toilet kit, a pigskin writing portfolio, a new duffle bag, cookies, fudge, and a candy horse for a joke present, and a bag of pretzels because Tad was such a pig about them.

Fortunately, the expressman called for the boxes that noon. If he had waited till Monday, it might have seemed a mockery to send them. The gay greeting cards would have sounded satirical: 'Merry, merry Christmas,' indeed! 'May you be very gay when you wear this.' And, worst of all, on Amy's copper jewelry, 'May this be the happiest of your twenty-one years.'

As it was, the cartons went their way, chockful of Christmas and of family affection for the girl at school and the boy at camp, both hungry for home, in spite of study and fun and hard work and daring and danger round the corner.

Sunday came, as lovely as Friday and Saturday. A high fog veiled the blue sky when Kim and Sue set out for church; and high fog mornings always exhilarated Sue. The church was the one Emily Andrews attended, and Jimmy Boyd, Kim's oldest friend. All four young people sang in the choir.

Sue loved sitting there in the reverent hush, cloaked, like all the other singers, young and old, in the flowing vestments that made them anonymous parts of the whole. Sometimes she listened to Mr. Clemons, their minister. When she did not listen, his kindly, earnest voice made a pleasant warp for the darting shuttle of her thoughts: 'I could pleat that scrumptious lace collar of mine and make a jabot like Miss Avery's, to wear with my navy suit. Did Kim make me a necklace? I hinted hard enough. I hope it was silver. The turquoise I set in Em's copper bracelet will look slick with her hair and eyes. I wonder what Em means to give me. I wish he'd send me a Christmas card. Is it just because Dad and Mom are so stiff with him that he never comes? Or is it because our fathers don't like each other? Like Romeo and Juliet — or does he think because they're poor and their house is shabby —— Maybe I'm just kidding myself, though. Maybe he looks at other girls that way, out between his thick lashes. And those valentines — how many years? — might not have come from him at all. Just because he carved a heart around my initials when we were kids —— If only he'd send me a Christmas card, I'd know he still thought about me ——'

'And I make myself sick, mooning about him the way I do,' she thought angrily. But still she could see him whenever her mind had leisure, not very tall, but straight and powerful, with confident broad shoulders and the ruddy face of an outdoor man, and with his own way of squinting his eyes almost shut when he grinned ——

Sue came back from her thoughts only in time to stand with the rest as they rustled to their feet for the minister's sounding syllables, 'And now may the great Shepherd of the sheep, who brought again ——' and to settle back once more as Mr. Clemons went down to the communion table and his deacons came up from the pews, the tall deacon, the small one, the broad ones and the average ones, and all, Sue thought, resembling each other, as if being deacons stamped them with the same mold.

The lifted-up, peaceful feeling communion always gave Sue did not interfere with her keen hunger. Today the morning was perfected by the crisp brown fragrance of roasting chicken that met her and Kim when they opened the door at home.

Father emerged from drifts of Los Angeles Sunday paper and came smiling to the table.

'The preacher asked after you, Dad,' Sue reproached him, flipping her napkin to her lap.

He shook his head, smiling. 'Sunday sickness, maybe. Very tired. Your mother and I will try to go tonight.'

He was a small man, smaller than any of his children, and behind his large glasses his bright eyes were rayed with smile wrinkles. Except for his hair, climbing up and back from his temples, he was like a round-faced boy. But it was true that he had looked tired of late, Sue thought.

At sight of the platter Mother set before him, he took up the carving knife and fork and leaned forward to peer pleasurably at the crusty surfaces, while his son and daughter waited with unconcealed zest. It was at this moment that the radio broke through its background of music to whistle and click the warning of a newscast.

'Why, what time is it?' Sue asked in surprise. 'I thought the Sunday concert was due.'

'Listen,' said Kim, motioning silence.

Into the startled quiet, the announcer's voice rang quick and sharp: 'Bulletin just in: Pearl Harbor bombed from the air. Extent of damage not yet known. U.S. fleet believed destroyed. Invasion of West Coast feared. Keep tuned to KFI for further bulletins.'

Sue's face stiffened as under a bitter wind, and Kim's lips and nostrils looked pinched and bloodless. The teapot came down softly on the center of its stand, but the carving knife clattered against the platter.

'It was the Nazis,' Kim said shrilly.

No one replied, and he pushed more words against their breathless silence. 'It has to be the Germans. Because, look, the diplomatic conversations are still going on at Washington. The conversations between us and the Japanese, Dad. Dad, it couldn't be the Japanese.'

Mr. Ohara took out his handkerchief and wiped his gray face.

'Dad!' Kim persisted, 'Japanese are — gentlemen.'

Father moistened his lips. 'Japan has changed — war-mad like Germany. But surely not the common people.'

'When you visited it you said ——'

'That was 1930.' Father's voice creaked. 'Yes, it was as beautiful as we had heard. But eleven years can change things.'

'Beautiful and kind,' Sue put in. 'Kind.'

Across her mind flashed pictures Father had brought home, on paper or in words: scarlet bridges amid trailing willow and wisteria; smiling little girls toeing in on high clogs; and together with these pictures lovely things an aunt had sent them from Kobe, lacquered and painted, delicate with crustings of gold, smelling exotic ——

'I always hated their soldier business, though,' Kim blurted out. 'Young kids brought up to glorify war.'

'Try another station, Son,' Father said.

The next newscast was saying, 'Casualties heavier than first supposed. Japanese in Honolulu said to have aided bombers.'

Groaning aloud, Kim smashed his fist down on the button that turned off the current.

Sue did not know how long they sat there, switching the radio on and off, while the untasted dinner grew cold. They were roused by Skippy, barking in the hall.

'Why, the bell's ringing,' Sue said dully.

She followed Kim dizzily, her ears buzzing as if she were in some faraway world, and was in time to catch the small figure that lurched into the hallway. Still numbly, Sue looked from the car at the curb to the round little face of Tomi Ito, her schoolmate. Tomi caught at Sue with shaking hands.

Though a part of today's fantasy, Tomi's coming seemed to waken Sue. The Itos were one of the Japanese farm families who sent their children to Cordova to high school. When Jiro Ito was graduated, two years earlier, he was one of the best-liked boys in his class. His sister Tomi was very different, a small, unnoticed shadow, hardly changed from the old Japanese pattern. Sue had never been drawn to the soft, submissive Tomi, but on Jiro's account she had befriended her, and now the girl's blanched face, her evident need, roused Sue's protectiveness, steadying her.

'Tomi! What on earth?'

'Didn't you heard?' Tomi stammered, her English lapsing with panic.

'It may not even be true. But anyway, it isn't you, Tomi. Good grief, it isn't you.'

'But the peoples.——' Tomi's teeth chattered — 'We come into town for spending afternoon, and a gang, it crowd around us and say things. Only tough boys, but they ——'

'Wasn't Jiro along?' Kim demanded.

Tomi caught back her sobs. 'Jiro answer them and some boy throw rocks. Jiro, he was knock' out. So we get him in car and I thought to come here. Where else?'

'Is he all right now? Jiro?' Sue asked with a quick-drawn breath.

Tomi nodded. 'He waking up and saying O.K.'

'They must come in,' Sue said, with an uneasy glance toward the dining room. 'And, Tomi, don't be upset. You're an American citizen, like anybody else. Like Kim and me. You can't help what those horrid Japanese war lords do ——'

Though Tomi was still trembling, her face had relaxed under Sue's words. But as the girls turned toward the door to invite the rest of the Itos in, they both stopped, speechless. Two men had come, unheard, to the threshold, and in that small town even Sue knew that they were F.B.I. men. One of them took the pipe from his mouth, glancing at the young people with a keen kindliness. 'Is Mr. Ohara in?' he asked.

Father came quickly, looking smaller than ever, and ushered the callers into the living room.

Again Tomi's face twisted with fear. Why not? How could Sue's words console her? Sue herself felt suddenly shelterless in this icy storm. Here were she and Kim, American-born; as American as baseball — ice-cream cones — swing music. No, as American as the Stars and Stripes. Here they were, American from their hearts out to their skins. But their skins were not American. Their skins were opaque, their hair was densely black, their eyes were ever so little slanted.

And their names were Sumiko and Kimio.

3

DOUBT IS THE BLACKEST SHADOW

Sue and Kim went out to the car with Tomi. Mr. Ito was already fidgeting behind the wheel. Evidently he, too, had recognized the callers.

Through Sue's numbness the sight of Jiro crashed like a blow. He was pulling himself up against the seat, hiding his forehead with a reddening handkerchief, and for an instant his face was empty of laughter. It was the first time Sue remembered seeing it so. Then it crinkled in its characteristic way, the lashes tangling and a corner of the mouth quirking up as if he were laughing at her, the world, himself.

'Hi, Susie!' he said. 'Aren't I a lively corpse?'

Sue smiled back, flushing as she unclenched her fists and smoothed out the tight lines in her brow. She had never told even Kim that this, from her childhood, had been The Boy in her small world.

'I suppose you — won't come in?' she asked rustily. 'Just for a drink and to put an antiseptic on your forehead?'

'We'd give you swell first aid,' Kim seconded her.

'Better we get along home,' said Mr. Ito, glancing toward the living-room window and a tall figure inside it.

Jiro nodded. 'This is nothing. I've had it a lot worse in football. But thanks all the same.'

The Ito car drove away, and Sue thought, as she went back into the house with Kim, how queer it was to see Jiro with his typically Japanese parents.

During her freshman and sophomore years he had been junior and senior. With a secret warmth of admiration she had watched him walk the school halls, carry the

15

pigskin, dribble the basketball, all with the becoming
slight swagger of the man who does everything well and
still has the liking of his group.

Set amidst his family, Sue thought with a contraction
of the heart, he was a different person. Or was the difference only superficial? And would Father and Mother
ever see him as she did?

Sue and Mrs. Ohara carried dinner from the table and
tidied the kitchen, Kim mechanically following them to
and fro. Nose on paws, Skippy lay anxiously watching
his people, while long shivers rippled the loose hide on his
small body.

Presently Father stood in the doorway and asked in a
high, toneless voice, how would it be if the three of them
went over to the Andrewses' for a little call?

Sue stammered, 'Those men? Have they gone?'

'They are not quite through discussing matters,'
Father said precisely. 'Just as well you go.'

They stayed two hours at the Andrewses' and relaxed
enough to listen to the radio and discuss the situation
with Emily and her mother. Yet always Father and the
F.B.I. men ran underneath Sue's thoughts. And when
Father telephoned, 'All right you come now if you wish,'
the Oharas started up like coiled springs suddenly let go.

At home the first thing Sue noticed was the scent of
tobacco. Neither Father nor Kim smoked, and the odor
of Tad's cigarettes had disappeared since his enlistment
a year ago. With nothing but cake and lemonade between
her and breakfast, Sue had begun to feel hungry, but the
acrid odor of tobacco in the kitchen took her appetite.

'Imagine Mother leaving cabinet drawers open,' she
commented to Kim, slamming two of them shut.

'Not Mother,' Kim said bleakly.

With a startled glance at him, Sue pelted upstairs to

her room. There the same smell tinged the air. She
dropped the lid of her desk. The pigeonholes were too
neat, as if the crammed-in letters had been taken out,
stacked on a skillful palm, and slid back into place.

Sue stood before the little old desk that had been her
mother's, and felt her body stiffen as if again in that cold
wind. For a moment this did not seem like her safe, dear
room, with a picture of Lincoln on one wall, the boy
Christ on another, Fujiyama on a third. Strange, sudden
men had violated it, fingered her possessions — hunting
for what?

Before Sue reached Emily's house on her way to school
next morning, Gloria Kane came running to overtake her
and linked an arm in hers. Gloria's blue eyes were solemn.

'Sue, you mustn't feel too bad about this mess,' she
cried breathlessly. 'Nobody blames you.'

While Sue tried to think what to say, a boy classmate
scudded past, waving a friendly arm. 'Chin up, Susie!'
he called. 'We all know you're O.K.'

It was a relief to have Emily fall in step beside her,
matter-of-factly. From everyone else came anxious
words of sympathy and trust. In one room the teacher
drummed her desk with nervous fingers and reminded
her classes that Pearl Harbor was the work of Japanese
militarists and had no bearing on American citizens of
Japanese blood.

Sue tried to smile her gratitude, but her mouth was
curiously stiff. Afterward she sat with chin in hands,
hair swinging forward and curtaining her face, while she
read a page of history over and over without taking in the
sense of it. Yesterday she had not realized how fully she
and Kim were involved — they, the native-born children
of citizens. In spite of the Shadow, she had felt secure in

her popularity with teachers and schoolmates — had felt
that she was one of them.

And now it was clear that she was not one of them.
Their very anxiety to reassure her showed that there was
need of reassurance. It put them on one side of the line
and Kim and her on the other.

Emily's father was a Scotchman, Peter Lucca's came
from Italy, Gretta Anderson's from Norway, Elsa Schonberg's from Germany. Yet these four were not Scotch-
American, Italo-American, Norwegian-American, Ger-
man-American; no, they were simply American.

Kim and Sue, on the contrary, born in this town of
parents who were Hawaiian-born American citizens, Kim
and Sue were Japanese-American. And what could
change their standing? Nothing, so long as their faces kept
their Oriental cast.

Sue clicked her compact open inside her history book
and studied that face of hers fiercely. She had always
regretted her chubbiness, but she had not minded her
face. The heavy blue-black hair set off its heart shape
admirably; the fine-grained ivory skin was like her mother's, as also was the mouth; the thin upper lip drew down
quaintly when she spoke, and an unexpected space between her upper teeth gave piquancy to her smile. Her
eyes were like her father's, wide-set and well opened;
and they were lustrous with youth. She hated the face;
hated it. If it were not for that face, she would be as
American as Emily. For the first time in her school life
Sue put her head down on the desk and wept.

The next days brought air-mail letters from Amy —
Emiko — and Tad — Tadashi, asking if all were well with
the family. The family wrote comforting replies. They
did not mention the F.B.I. search of the house. What
need to trouble the distant boy and girl?

For the most part, Cordova was kind. For twenty-five years Father and Mother had lived there. They belonged to the Baptist Church, and Father was a Rotarian and a respected business man. Being the only Japanese inside the town, the Oharas had been judged more on their worth as individuals than if they had been members of a close-packed colony, like most of the West Coast Japanese.

There were worrying rumors. Dispatches charged that Japanese-Americans had interfered with rescue work in Honolulu, blocking the way with their own cars. Contrary dispatches said the Japanese-Americans had labored side by side with the whites, aiding in the rescues, and that their cars, photographed 'blockading the way,' had in fact been bombed to a standstill by the raiders while their owners were using them to help wounded Americans. Finally Honolulu's Chief of Police issued a sworn statement that there had been no known sabotage or espionage by any Japanese-American in Honolulu.

Still a new unfriendliness grew up along the Coast. One day Father came home from the shop, looking unusually worn and anxious.

'Matter?' he answered Mother's query. 'Well, they are talking of moving our people from vital military areas. Along the coast and near harbors and military camps.'

'You don't mean — a town like this?' Sue asked.

Father nodded.

'Then why not the Italian-Americans?' Kim cried. 'Or the Germans?'

'Yes; ten times as many Italians on the Atlantic Coast as Japanese out here. But they say it is harder to make sure whether we are loyal.'

'But surely not American citizens?'

Again Father nodded. 'The J.A.C.L. may be able to

help.' J.A.C.L. was Japanese-American Citizens' League. 'They talk of bringing cases to court, to test whether evacuation is constitutional. But it may be better for us to evacuate ourselves.'

Mother stared down at the teacup she was filling, her face immobile as an old Japanese print. 'Why does she have to look so Japanese?' Sue thought bitterly, and then was softened by remorse as she saw her mother's hands shake.

'But not — not us?' Kim's voice was flat.

'We are no different from hundreds of others.'

'Where would we go?' Sue gasped.

'Perhaps we could buy a farm somewhere inland ——'

'I suppose it's the few disloyal Japanese that have stirred up all this,' Kim muttered. 'They say some of them had hidden maps. And ammunition and short-wave radios.'

'Mr. Kimura,' Sue admitted. 'They took him to a detention camp, and a magazine article says he's in the Black Dragon Society and the Japanese Navy, and that his fishing boat's nothing but a blind.'

'You'd best break up your airplane models,' Mr. Ohara said abstractedly. 'The F.B.I. men noticed them. And your chemistry outfit in the basement.'

Kim stared. Years ago he had filled the house with models, and the best ones still hung from the ceiling of his room, so that he had to duck under them now that he had grown tall. Something of their old preciousness still hovered round them. 'I — won't break them,' he said. 'I'll give them to Bobby Clemons. And I better take the chemicals over to Jimmy. Jim and I laid out two hundred bucks ——'

'Could it be some innocent thing like that with the Kimuras, too?' Sue put in hopefully. She had gone clambering all over that trim polished craft with Kim and the Kimura boys and girls.

Mr. Ohara said: 'No, the F.B.I. are pretty smart; not easily fooled. But nations at war build up hate so that their people will fight. In the First World War they told stories about the Germans. In this one it's the Japanese.'

'If it's true about the Kimuras,' Kim said in a strangled voice, 'I'd have been willing to turn them in to the F.B.I. myself. I like Saburo Kimura, but I'd turn him in like a rat.'

'You will sell the house, the nursery, the shop?' Mother asked tautly.

'Will? Better say "Would." Those who might pay a fair price have no money. Those with money offer a cent on the dollar.' Father stopped, smiling toward the kitchen door.

Emily came in and perched on a chair near the table. 'You said — sell?' she asked. 'You're — moving?'

'It may be necessary,' Mr. Ohara replied.

'If only Daddy had the money,' Emily quavered. 'He'd buy your business, I know he would. Or lease it.'

'But he is a physician,' Mr. Ohara objected.

'For her sister Marian, she means,' Sue put in.

Emily nodded, her bright hair an aureole around her flushed face. 'Marian finishes this semester. Horticulture at Berkeley, Mr. Ohara. I know Dad would love to have her start business here; but he isn't the kind of doctor with loads of money.'

Into Sue's mind crept a sudden hateful thought, 'Maybe even Emily wouldn't so much mind our being driven out if her family profited by it.' Then she grew hot with shame, looking at Emily's auburn lashes, wet into dark spikes by the tears that brimmed her eyes. 'Can it be I, Sue Ohara,' she asked herself, 'holding such ugly suspicions?'

Perhaps this was the worst thing about the sorry up-
heaval: this new fear; this doubt even of her friends; yes,
this faint wing-brush of a doubt of Father.

And as the weeks went by, Father drew more and more
into himself. December passed, and January, with the
business still unsold and Father increasingly silent.

He had changed into old clothes and was working dog-
gedly in the yard one evening, while Kim helped him, and
Sue hurried with the dinner dishes so that she might join
them. The outdoors called her urgently, for spring had
come, and flowering almonds, peaches and apricots were
in fragrant bloom.

Sue halted with a fistful of forks bristling from her dish-
towel. Outside she heard deep, slow voices mingling
with Father's high, questioning one. Into the kitchen
came Mr. Ohara, the F.B.I. men close on his heels.

'Do not be alarmed,' Father said, in a voice he tried to
keep down to normal pitch. 'It is only for questioning ——'

'No, there's no occasion for worry, Mrs. Ohara,' one
of the men put in courteously. 'We're just taking your
husband down to headquarters ——'

Father looked down at his ragged sweater, his house
shoes. 'I go and change,' he said, turning to the door.

'Come as you are, Mr. Ohara. It's only business.'

They were kind but immovable, these men, and behind them stood a Government that seemed suddenly
hostile to the Oharas. Father washed his hands at the
sink and brushed down his thin hair with the flat of his
palm.

'Good-bye for the present,' he told his family, smiling
mechanically. Then quick steps, the slam of a car door,
the roar of a motor.

All night the house waited restlessly, and it was barely

light next morning when Mrs. Ohara opened the doors wide to the fresh air and the mockingbird songs. Skippy dashed out, sniffed his way along the walk to the curb, then trotted back and tried it over.

'There are always dishes to wash,' Sue observed after the half-eaten breakfast.

'A blessing,' Mother agreed. 'Life without dishes to wash, when the hard things come ——'

Noon passed, and still no word from Father. Each time the young Oharas raced to answer telephone or door-bell, Sue's heart tangled in her throat. Once it was a reporter; once Emily. But at last when Sue said, 'The Ohara residence,' the voice of one of the F.B.I. men was in her ear.

'Miss Ohara? Your father would like you to pack him a bag ——'

'A — bag?' Sue asked huskily.

'He said a good suit, underclothes, night-clothes, toilet-kit. That sort of thing. He prefers that you and your brother bring it down.'

It was too unreal to be painful, that ride down to the jail with Father's bag. But Father was real, smaller than ever in his rumpled clothes.

'Father,' Sue whispered tensely, 'they haven't — hurt you?'

Father looked astonished. 'After all, Daughter,' he said dryly, 'this is America.'

'*Is* it?' Kim muttered.

Father looked through his bag and found that Mother had remembered everything, even the soda-mints he needed after eating. 'You will take good care of your mother while I am away,' he said, slipping a mint into his mouth.

'*Away?*'

'They are taking me to Sacramento. Do not look so alarmed. What could happen? Better get Wing Lin to look after the nursery. The boy will manage the shop if your mother supervises him. And perhaps Amy and Tad need not know till I am home once more.'

Soon the young Oharas were out in the afternoon sunshine again, and surprised to find it still bright and normal. When they reached the house, the daily paper lay on the porch steps. Kim snapped off the rubber band and opened it out.

'Sue!' he ejaculated, and jerked it toward her as she turned with her hand on the doorknob.

Unbelievingly she stared at the headlines. CORDOVA JAP HALED TO PRISON, the black letters shouted. The two stood chilled in the afternoon sunshine, reading the garbled story.

'Plane models — chemicals ——' Kim stuttered. 'Short-wave radio — whose isn't? — fine cameras — I suppose they mean my last Christmas Argus.'

'How could they?' Sue whispered.

Kim flapped the paper angrily. 'This isn't the F.B.I. They've got too much sense. But the paper's had it in for Dad ever since the editor's brother went bust in the florist business here. That's all there is to this.'

He paused. A woman was coming up their walk, unrolling a sheaf of magazines. She stopped at the foot of the steps and stared up at them.

'Are you Chinese?' she demanded.

'No, ma'am, Japanese-Americans,' Kim said. 'Is there something we can do for you?' he added, when she still stared wordlessly.

The woman rolled up the magazines decisively. 'Do for me?' she asked fiercely. 'You? Can you bring back my boy? No, you murdered him at Pearl Harbor. You

— you smirking Japs! But we had it coming. We let you work your way in, two-faced and treacherous ——

'Oh, stare!' she broke off, her voice shaken with passion and tears. 'Stare like innocent babies. If you were so straight as all that, you'd have the decency to go back where you came from ——'

After the woman had clicked down the street, the brother and sister still stood petrified. At last Sue stumbled into the house ahead of Kim and went straight to her room, where she sat on the edge of the bed staring before her. Her life seemed hanging motionless, the blood stopped in her veins, no breath entering her flattened lungs.

She could hear Kim's voice downstairs, and presently her mother came in, with a tray of tea and toast. Not looking at Sue, Mrs. Ohara set down the tray and came and pulled Sue's sweater over her head as if she were a doll; stood her up; said, 'Undress now, Daughter. Slip into bed. Drink the hot tea.'

'That terrible woman! I can't seem to get my breath,' Sue said heavily.

'Poor woman,' her mother said, and her eyes sought the window with a far look; as far as Tad, maybe.

'Tomorrow will be better,' she went on. 'And words will never again hurt you so. It was because this was the first hatred you had felt. To be despised — it does something dreadful inside you. But it will be better tomorrow.'

Sue slept fitfully, waking with a jump to stare at the cold thin disk of the moon and the shapes of peppers and palms outside her window. How could they look the same as ever, when all else in life was so changed?

4

AN END OF TEARS

In that incomplete house, fourteen days and nights limped by without word from Father. Then came a letter postmarked Bismarck, North Dakota. Mother held it incredulously in her hands. The end was closed with a strip of cellophane, and across one corner a red stamp said, CENSORED, WAR DEPARTMENT.

Father — *Father* — had been interned.

Already questions had been creeping into Tad's and Amy's letters. *You folks aren't getting downhearted, I hope*, Amy wrote. *Your letters are too darn cheerful. Goodness, people can't help recognizing that we're as much Americans as anybody. But why doesn't Dad write? Most dads let the mothers do the writing, but he's always been a duck about it.*

Tad wrote, *What's eating Dad? Or is business so good he can't even scratch a line to his eldest? I was afraid our places might be getting boycotted. Glad if they aren't, but Dad might manage a p.c.*

In another week their letters grew more urgent: *Dear Father, ARE YOU THERE? WHAT HAVE I DONE?* And, *Say, Gov, you aren't down with hydrophobia or something? Then for Pete's sake write.*

By that time the censored mail was coming from Bismarck, and the home Oharas composed casual replies. Father was fine; he was awfully sorry ('Darn tootin' he's sorry,' Kim growled) that unexpected business had kept him from writing even to Tad, his eldest; even to Papa's Pet, Amy.

The elaborate excuses failed. One evening when Sue

answered the telephone she heard her sister's voice, as clear as if from Los Angeles: 'Sue, let me speak to Father.'

Sue thought fast. 'Oh, Amy, hello! How marvelous! But won't Mother do? Father's out of town. Business ——'

Amy said: 'Sue, don't stall. Has anything happened to Dad? Since when have I been such a baby I couldn't be told things? Where is my father?'

'He's fine, and being taken good care of,' Sue answered, gulping. 'He's — he's in a detention camp.'

Amy said thickly, 'I'll come straight home, Sue.'

Mother had pressed close, listening. She took the telephone from Sue and spoke. 'No, Emiko. Your father wishes you to finish the school year and get work there in the East. In that way you need not come to camp if the rest of us go. You will not grieve us by disobedience, Daughter.'

Faintly Sue could hear her sister's shocked voice: 'But what grounds? Why, *Father* —?'

'We cannot imagine. But all is sure to come straight in time. We must say good-bye, Emiko.'

No, they could not imagine what Father had ever done to incur suspicion. Their pastor, Mr. Clemons, suggested that his visit to Japan ten years earlier might have implied too keen an interest in that country. Doctor Andrews wondered whether it was his asking a member of the Japanese consulate to speak at a Rotary meeting. Both said, comfortingly, that the F.B.I. would uncover the truth, in time.

In time; but would it be in time? If Father were not soon freed, it would be too late for him to sell his business. For wholesale eviction was becoming a certainty. Voluntary evacuation was not satisfactory. Perhaps six thousand undertook it, and most of them were like children used only to their own neighborhood and panic-stricken in the wilderness east of the Coast.

Some made a place for themselves, but others pressed from town to town, not allowed to settle anywhere. The Oharas heard of carloads of Japanese met by townspeople with rifles, ordering them on, refused food in restaurants, gasoline at service stations. Sue saw them in her dreams, frail grandparents and frightened children among them.

'We'll get us a farm,' Kim said stoutly.

'But we can't sell our property here,' Sue objected.

'I bet it won't take Dad long to sell it, once he gets home,' said Kim. 'Even if he has to lose on it, he'll be so glad to get a new start somewhere ——'

Once he got home ——

And then one day when Sue was helping her mother in the shop, Kim brought the news. 'You can just quit holding your breath,' he announced savagely. 'Dad can't get home in time.'

Sue's heart lurched. Had they found Father guilty of some pro-Japan activity? Could it be possible? 'How do you mean?' she asked, stopping with feet braced in the act of lifting a heavy jar of roses.

'We're frozen.' Kim grated out the word.

Mrs. Ohara, arranging acacia branches in a blue basket for the window, dropped her hands. 'Frozen?'

'In a strip one hundred miles inland, the length of the Pacific Coast. We're to stay put till March 19.'

'Citizens, too?' Sue asked. Her momentary relief about Father gave place to another misery. *Jiro.* As long as they were within a few miles of each other, doing business in the same stores, even the strange enmity of parents could not prevent their seeing one another now and then. But if they were all uprooted, then what chance would there be?

'Citizens, too,' Kim was saying. 'It's been the yellow newspapers and flashy magazines. And people like the Cordova editor, who saw a chance readymade to drive us out and have the field for themselves. It's poisoning all California. Gosh, I've felt it even here. Folks that always took us for granted, why, they look at me as if I'd suddenly put on one of those hateful Tojo faces in the cartoons, all teeth and goggles.'

'And then what?' Sue asked, in a faraway voice, still standing astride the roses.

'The Government's building temporary camps, and on March 19 they'll begin moving us into them. Back in the dark ages they evacuated Eastern Indians, and that trek was called the "Trail of Tears." This'll be our Trail of Tears.'

Sue stared out through the open door at the nursery. She had always thought it the prettiest in the world. Acres of flowers, like skeins of embroidery floss, shading from light to dark in red, in yellow, in lavender; baby forests of shrubs, evergreens, other trees. The very soil looked happy, as if it knew itself loved, fed, tended.

Now they were to leave it, and for what unknown place? What place far from friends? And Father's kind, work-rough fingers, how would they endure longer idleness, longer separation from the good earth?

'I met Reverend Clemons,' Kim put in. 'He said we were welcome to store our goods in the top of his garage.'

'We can't — take our things?'

'Well, just figure it out for yourself,' Kim said harshly.

Hardly had the news of coming evacuation been made public when a secondhand dealer came to the Ohara door, his eyes peering covetously over their shoulders. He would pay top prices, he told Kim. Kim asked what would be top price for their new living-room furniture, for

instance? The dealer tilted a lounge chair to determine
its construction, appraised the couch, the tables, and
named a figure that sent the blood rushing angrily to
Kim's face.

'Tomi says the secondhand men looked over their house-
hold goods and offered them twenty dollars for the lot,'
Sue said, when Kim had closed the door on their caller.

'And a car dealer offered them fifty for their Buick, the
only valuable thing they've got,' Kim added.

'But one of the worst things was that a lawyer — a
white lawyer — came to Mr. Ito and offered to fix up
papers for them so that they wouldn't get interned. For
a hundred-dollar fee,' said Sue.

'Did they fall for it?' Kim inquired.

'No, Jiro was too smart, Tomi said.'

'Sure Jiro's smart,' Kim said teasingly. 'You always
did think so, Sis.'

'Your humor is misplaced, my son,' Mrs. Ohara said
stiffly. 'The Itos are not people who would interest Sue
in any way such as you suggest.'

'Excuse me, Mother,' Kim said with a frown, 'but that
sounds downright Japanese. They don't come any better
than Jiro. Ambitious, too. If his old man wasn't a close-
fisted failure, Jiro'd be studying medicine right now.'

It wasn't often that a young Ohara spoke so bluntly to
a parent. Mrs. Ohara compressed her lips, then said
calmly that it was wonderful to think they would not have
to sell all their possessions for nothing.

'The minister is kind, letting us store our things there,'
she murmured, looking at the glowing maple and walnut
of her beloved home. 'Almost all the church people
have been good ——'

Mother had been an occasional churchgoer, easily kept
at home by rain or by a roast in the oven. Now she went

every Sunday. Within the church the Oharas were for
a little while walled away from the bitter wind.

'Why don't we take the minister some of our plants?'
Mrs. Ohara went on thoughtfully. 'This house may stand
empty for months, and the flowers ——'

To the Oharas, growing things were children. Evening
after evening the family worked at taking up fuchsias and
Martha Washington geraniums, camellias, double be-
gonias; taking barrowfuls to the Andrewses, carfuls to the
Clemonses, basketfuls to the neighbors. Skippy would
run barking around them, or sit watching, head cocked,
or help dig with rapid front paws.

'How'll Skippy stand moving?' Sue queried one day,
sitting back on her heels and staring at him.

'I'll build him a carrying-box,' Kim planned, surveying
Skippy with a tape-measure frown. 'How'd you like
that?'

'He'll hate being shut up,' Sue said with a sigh.

'Dogs and flowers ——' Kim observed, cutting carefully around a precious flowering peach. 'I'm not going
to feel half so sick over leaving the house empty, so long
as we won't have to think of these babies dying of neglect.
But the business is something else again. Wing can't
carry it indefinitely. I suppose in the end we'll have to
let it go to that guy who made us the offer. What he'd
give would do a little better than cover outstanding bills,
Dad says. But I've got the darndest hunch that that
buyer is only acting for the newspaper editor's brother.
Gosh, would such a mean cuss take the right care of plants
and trees?'

He fell silent. 'He's thinking of Father's orchids,' Sue
thought.

She said, 'What we do we've got to do quick. Do you
realize how close the end is, Kim?'

Kim rolled Skippy over and tussled with him in the way the dog loved, and then jumped up and brushed the moist earth from his knees. 'Right now let's be quick about setting this flowering peach over at the Andrewses'. Touchy to move it when it's in bloom, but we'll get it in so quick it won't know it's been evacuated.'

Emily and her sister greeted them eagerly, and Marian helped with hands that had already learned some skill. 'You've made this yard lovelier than ever,' she said. 'Kim, have you found a buyer for your business?'

'We've found a man we can give it to.'

Marian studied a feathery acacia twig. 'Would you think I was crazy —?' she began. 'Gladys Phillips and I have done pretty well in horticulture, but of course we're nothing but inexperienced girls. Wing Lin's had plenty of experience, though ——'

The young Oharas stared, and Emily giggled and squeezed Sue. 'They could do it, I know they could. With Wing Lin. He's the honestest Chinese, and the deepest ——'

'Are you offering —?' Kim stuttered ——

'Oh, not to buy it,' Marian hastened. 'But why couldn't Glad and I be kind of apprentices to Wing Lin? We'd take what pay your dad thought was right. Or maybe a small minimum wage and a percentage of profits. We can write him about that. But if you can't dispose of the business without losing practically the whole thing, wouldn't it be better for us to carry on until you all came home again?'

'It might be a long pull,' Sue said huskily.

Marian squared her shoulders. 'You can count on us to do our durndest till the cows come home,' she said.

March came, with every day so full that the Oharas must stretch it at both ends: go to bed exhausted at mid-

night, rise unrested at six. The second semester of school
was more than half over; neglected assignments must be
completed, daily lessons given some attention. And between the rush of school and business, the Oharas were
packing their possessions.

'I had no idea we had accumulated so much,' Mrs.
Ohara said. 'Sue, these cartons labeled "Sumiko,"
"Emiko," are linens I've always meant for your hope
chests.'

Sue nodded absently. 'It's the dickens to decide what
to keep and what to chuck. Emily's going to keep some
special ones for me, Mom. My cloisonné toilet set, and
my dolls, and my diaries. But it's things like these ——'
She was holding a Memory Book, fat and shaggy with
programs, invitations, snapshots. She shoved it aside to
finger a crêpe-paper fairy costume, with huge butterfly
wings. 'I suppose it's silly to pack this. You made it for
me when I was six, and I always did think my little girl
would love to dress up in it.'

They packed, burned, crammed burlap bags for the
Goodwill. They stacked small boxes neatly under the
eaves in the minister's barn-garage. The house grew bare
and echoed eerily under their hurrying feet.

They would be allowed only hand luggage when they
went to the Assembly Centers. They kept suitcases open
in their rooms, putting something in one day and taking
it out in favor of something else the next.

Kim used his spare moments to make Skippy's carrying-
case, Jimmy helping. It was shingled with left-over
asbestos shingles and had a glass window: a beautiful
little house, though so heavy Sue said they'd have to hook
it behind their car like a trailer. When Sue put in Skippy's
favorite pillow, patched and faded, he stepped through
the door and curled up with a sigh, his eye still watchful,
to see that this was not a trick to go riding without him.

On the seventh of April an official folder was distributed to the Japanese of the Oharas' district, from the 'Western Defense Command and Fourth Army Wartime Civil Control Administration.' It told the evacuees what to do and what to take with them for use in the Assembly Center where they would go before their removal to the more permanent relocation camp. Recognizing that unscrupulous people had taken advantage of the Japanese in the disposal of their personal property, the Government offered them free storage. And for further instructions heads of families were to come to the Civil Control Stations during the next two days.

Forlornly proud, young Kim went to the station.

'Be sure to find out about Skippy,' Sue said, going out to the car with him.

'It's pure bosh to think they wouldn't let us take Skippy,' Kim declared, pulling out the clutch.

'Well, you know what Ai said about her police pup.'

Ai was a Los Angeles friend who had already gone to one of the Assembly Centers.

'She didn't know how to work it,' said Kim, scowling as if Sue were to blame, and jerking the car into motion.

An hour later he strode moodily into the house.

'Well, what about it?' Sue asked.

'What about what?'

'Oh — *men!* You know perfectly well. What about Skippy?'

Kim said levelly, 'No pets to be taken.'

The Oharas stared at each other and at Skippy.

'Why, they might as well say you couldn't take us, Mother,' Sue protested, the tears blocking up her nose. 'Skippy's like a person. He's an Ohara.'

'I bet Jimmy'd keep him,' Kim muttered.

'No, their cat. But Emily would.'

'We couldn't ask them,' Mrs. Ohara said decisively. 'A little old dog like Skippy makes too much work. I would not consent to the untidiness myself; but when you've had a pet fourteen years —— There are boarding kennels, though.'

'They aren't always kind to them,' Sue said, her voice still nasal with tears. 'Skippy wouldn't know what to think if he were treated like a — like a dog.'

'He wouldn't last long,' Kim said soberly.

Skippy knew he was being talked about, and he made a circuit of the three, dabbing at their ankles with a moist tongue to show his undying affection. Then he folded his hindquarters in the efficient sitting-down motion of a little dog, and sat in the center of the group, head cocked.

'But what is there left to do?' Sue demanded, dropping to her knees and scooping him up against her. Skippy growled and scrambled to the floor, but immediately jumped up to lick her ear in apology.

'Maybe only one kind thing,' said Mrs. Ohara.

Sue leaped to her feet, face contorted. 'No. I won't let you,' she whispered, and ran from the room.

In the end she did consent, and the handsome carrying-case became Skippy's casket. Emily came that afternoon and stayed with Sue till it was over.

'If we were kids we'd soothe our feelings by having a funeral,' Emily said, trying to laugh. 'Remember the canary? Mother was so shocked because we'd named it for you, and the little tombstone read, "Sue Ohara, Died January, 1933."'

'Where will we bury Skippy?' Sue wondered.

'Why not under our live oak?' Emily suggested. 'He loved to lie there in the shade.'

So they carried the dog-house over to the Andrews yard,

and Kim dug a deep hole in the leafy shadows. When they had smoothed the turf neatly over Skippy's catafalque, it was as if something more than Skippy were buried there. Sue stood up decisively, rubbing at her face with her two earth-stained hands.

'After all,' she said harshly, 'this is childish. We have bigger things to grieve about. Skippy was — he was only a dog. I won't cry about him again. I think I am through crying forever.'

5

MOVED OUT

Even when evacuation day came, Sue Ohara's eyes were dry. She would not have confessed to anyone how much easier it was to be stoic when she learned that the Ito family would be going to the same Assembly Center. And the hurry and rush of getting ready made the young Oharas forget, most of the time, that this was — for nobody knew how long — Last Day.

The last night Sue spent with Emily, and the girls talked till the small hours. Kim stayed with Jim Boyd, and Mrs. Ohara with the Clemonses. Then, after early breakfast, the Oharas met at their deserted house, where the car was packed and waiting in the locked garage.

With the house empty and the yard stripped of its choicest foliage and flowers, it was not so hard to say good-bye to home. Still, Sue did run upstairs for a last look through her bedroom window. The palms and pepper trees seemed woven with girlhood dreams. And she did stand and gaze a moment at the chubby heart and the

S.O. on the front walk. The cement of the new sidewalk had happened to be still wet, that day ten years ago when the twelve-year-old Jiro had come to their house with his father. He had carved the design deep, smiling at her through his thick lashes. The young Oharas did not know why he did not come to the house again, nor his father. They did not know why Mr. Ito was always too polite, and Father cool and stiff; nor whether their unfriendliness stemmed from that very day.

The hour of departure had been set for eight-thirty, and Cordova was just getting to work when the Oharas reached the town hall where they had been directed to meet. From farms, market gardens, fruit ranches, all around Cordova, the Japanese had gathered. A line of cars were drawn up at the curb, all but the Itos' big Buick and the Oharas' Dodge dingy workaday ones. The people who were going in buses sat on their bags and suitcases or drooped patiently above them.

It seemed like some strange going-away party, all blurred and distorted by Sue's excitement. She politely thanked Mrs. Clemons and the other church women, who were pouring hot coffee and passing puffy sugared doughnuts; but she hardly knew that she was eating and drinking. Still munching doughnuts, she and Emily drifted over to the Ito car and talked to Tomi, wedged into the back seat between her mother and younger sister, and to Jiro, behind the wheel.

'Look, Sue,' Emily cried, tugging at her arm, 'the gang ——'

Sue hung back, saying, 'You come, too, Tomi. And Jiro. It's kids from school.'

Jiro shook his head. 'It's your crowd, Susie. And Tomi's in too much of a funk. I can't convince her but what we're going to be dumped in a camp and left to starve.'

'Oh, Tomi, for goodness' sake! Well, we'll be seeing you.' Sue laughed protestingly, but Tomi's face was almost as white and frightened as it had been on Pearl Harbor Day.

And then Sue forgot Tomi as the dozen boys and girls swarmed around her, and around Kim. Gloria was there, and among the rest were Peter Lucca and Elsa Schonberg, who didn't have to be pulled up by the roots and dropped on new soil whether or not.

Now it was more than ever like a going-away party, with 'train-letters,' boxes of candy, a basket of goodies, a boutonnière — with everyone talking at once, with girls laughing artificially and boys pushing each other around.

Then the M.P.'s began to load people into the buses, and a tight, awkward silence seized the group of school-mates. The evacuees climbed quietly into the waiting vehicles, some with a heavy weariness, some stolidly, some with determined smiles. There was no outcry until one old woman pushed aside the hands helping her aboard, turned wildly toward Cordova, and uttered a sobbing, gulping cry.

Sue had a single glimpse of the old face, furrowed deep as a dried peach, the corded throat working convulsively. Then the two hands, like bundles of sticks, came up to hide that naked grief, and the woman's friends lifted her into the bus.

'She thinks she'll never see her home again. Likely she's been coming here to market since she was young,' Emily quavered, the tears running.

'Guess the clock's struck, Sis,' Kim said loudly, heartily — and the young people moved in a mass toward the car.

Hands thrust out to shake hers — Emily's wet face against her own — boys slapping Kim's back till he staggered ——

The gang breaking down in the middle of 'He's a jolly good fellow.' Mrs. Clemons starting 'God be with you till we meet again.' Pitching it too high. Mr. Clemons pitching it too low. The church people joining in, waveringly, voices thick with grief.

Just as the buses rumbled into motion and the song ended, a kindergartener leaned out of the window of a bus and piped to his teacher, 'See you in the morning, Mis' Jones!' just as he had done every day.

At that, all the determined smiles of church women and schoolgirls melted into weeping, and the boys ran alongside the Ohara car hiding their emotion with pointless jokes: 'Don't take any wooden nickels!' 'Write once in a while if you haven't too many dates!'

From the Ito car Jiro looked back and waved. His head was high and his eyes lost themselves behind his thick lashes. He seemed to signal, 'Adventure, Sue! Pioneers, remember!'

The caravan gained speed, and Sue screwed around to watch the throng at the town hall until the turn of a corner hid them from sight. Then she fixed her gaze on Cordova till they passed its limits and sped out along the highway. Heading the procession, bringing up the rear, weaving through it, keeping back other traffic, were the dusty jeeps, and the young M.P.'s in them shouted friendly directions, joked with the evacuee children, grinned or looked sympathetically sober. Sue's heart swelled with gratitude toward them.

'Since we've got to go, I'm sort of glad we're going to Santa Anita,' said Sue, trying to lift Kim's dejection.

Kim only growled.

'All these years I've wanted to see the races there,' Sue went on, vivaciously, 'and never dreamed I'd be living there some day. Swankiest race-track ——'

'Oh, dry up,' Kim begged with brotherly courtesy.

The ride was short. Within two hours the entourage slowed up, and Sue, peering out, could see that the buses were turning in at the Santa Anita entrance. Jiro grinned back at her, flipping a hand in mock awe at the tall, many-windowed façade, the lofty palms, the fountain. They had arrived.

Private cars were left at the entrance, where they would be cared for and sold for the owners. Sue saw Kim's hand linger on the wheel of their Dodge in a furtive caress. He had done his first driving in that car, and he would not see it again.

The Oharas lugged their bags inside and left them on tables where inspectors were opening the luggage. Behind the Ito family they filed past the doctor at the entrance, showing him their throats and their hands and then pushing on along the graveled walk.

'Barracks 15, Apartments A–2 and A–3, that's where we're assigned,' said Jiro. 'What about you folks?'

'Barracks 15, Apartment B–2,' Kim read from the page of instructions that had just been handed to his mother.

Sue felt herself flushing with pleasure. Jiro would be their neighbor, no matter how frosty Mother was looking about it. Jiro would be their neighbor, so it didn't matter much that there were only one or two familiar faces among those peering from stable doors and windows to watch the newcomers.

'And here we are,' said Jiro, striding ahead to throw open the Oharas' door. 'Welcome home!'

'Gosh,' said Kim, momentarily forgetting his gloom, 'must have been a prince of a horse to rate this. Reckon it was Whirlaway or Seabiscuit?'

'A horse's stall as big as my kitchen!' cried Mrs. Ohara.

'Doesn't smell like your kitchen,' said Sue.

The individual exercise yard had been walled up to make another room; an asphalt floor had been put in; the walls had been whitewashed; but the odor remained.

'Smells?' asked Jiro, from the half-door of the next stall. 'I can't smell anything. Too used to it, maybe.' Grinning, he gestured toward the small hallway between the stalls. 'This was where they forked in the hay. The former inmates just stuck their heads through these half-doors and got their grub. Service, what?'

'You make me hungry,' Sue said. 'And we don't have long to wait. Look: this sheet says, "Breakfast six-thirty, dinner eleven-thirty, supper four-thirty." Good grief!'

Kim said, 'At Alcatraz they wake the prisoners even earlier.'

'Surely they said cots and mattresses would be supplied,' Mother said anxiously, looking around the complete emptiness of the twenty-by-ten feet.

'Yes,' said Sue; 'and it isn't going to be so bad. In New York it's all the style to turn old barns into swanky houses. We'll be in fashion. But when will they let us have our bags?' she demanded of Jiro, as if he should know everything.

'Want to go see if they're ready?' he asked.

He and Kim, Tomi and Sue, walked back along the streets of stalls and stood watching the M.P.'s opening bundles and bags.

'Gosh,' said Kim, 'can't they take our word for it that we haven't any contraband?'

Without speaking, Jiro pointed at the cameras, the radios, the one or two knives the M.P.'s had tossed aside.

'Remember the Kimuras, Kim,' said Sue, adopting Jiro's easy attitude. 'Trouble is, they think we're all tricky, and we think we're all woolly white lambs. Really,

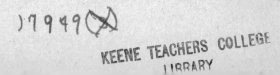

we're like any other bunch of folks. Lookit! Another camera!'

When they got back to their quarters with their ex-onerated luggage, they found that three cots had been delivered to the Oharas. When Mother and Sue had made them up with white sheets and the army blankets, even those cots gave the stalls a feeling of home.

'Almost dinnertime!' Jiro called, just as Sue plumped her pillow into place. 'And a fellow told me we'd have a plenty long wait if we weren't on time.'

A tremendous bang and clatter put a period to his words. 'Gong of the Blue Mess,' he added.

The Oharas and the Itos were soon part of the queue winding toward the mess-hall door. A kitchen boy whanged his battered dishpan a few more times, flourished his stick and vanished into the kitchen.

'Cowboy style, I take it,' said Jiro.

Inside the hall, the Itos and Oharas were engulfed in warm heavy food odors and the din of forks, spoons, tins. Presently they were balancing heaped plates and hunting a place at the tables. As they came to a vacant place, Mrs. Ohara hesitated outside the long backless bench.

Sue giggled. 'Turn sidewise,' she instructed, taking her mother's dishes. 'Put one foot over, like this. Now sit astraddle, so, and lift over your other foot. You don't have to blush so, Mom. Everybody's doing it. But it would be easier in slacks.'

The scraping of dishes at the end of the hall drowned conversation, but Sue was too engrossed in the endless file of diners to talk. Young people called to each other as they made their way down the crowded aisles between tables, fathers and mothers kept their children under their wings, older Japanese bowed rhythmically to ac-quaintances, or shuffled along blank-faced and silent.

Sue looked more than she ate, but Kim emptied his plate and stood in line for a second helping, coming home an hour after the others, because it had taken forty-five minutes to get to the serving table again.

The afternoon passed. There were letters to write. There were the first inoculations to take. There was the evening meal at half-past four.

For a while after supper the young people walked to and fro before their stalls. Here, withdrawn from the barbed wire which fenced the camp, and with other people walking, talking, laughing around them, the place did not feel abnormal. The difference showed itself when twilight thickened and the searchlights began to flash. Up and down the streets, across roofs, in at windows, played the hard white light. It swept across Sue's and Tomi's faces as they loitered before the Ohara door. Tomi ducked her head, shutting her eyes and mewing like a drenched kitten, and even Sue felt as if she were drowning in that bright relentless flood.

'This is like prison,' Sue thought desperately. 'Like the searchlights wheeling ceaselessly round Alcatraz ——'

Even without the lights, that first night would have been wakeful. The legs of the cots had sunk into the soft asphalt so that the beds tilted and wabbled. It was late before the day's heavy heat began to lift from the Ohara apartment; and in the row of stalls behind it where windows were fewer, babies whimpered and wailed till midnight. The partitions were thin, and Sue could hear Kiku Ito ask for a drink; could hear his mother say that no one had remembered to bring water from the hydrant several doors away. Twice an hour the neighbor on the Oharas' right wakened them with a magnificent sneeze; and from the stall that backed up against theirs came another set of coughs, laughs, squeakings of restless cots.

'My grief!' Sue muttered. 'I suppose all those other people can hear us breathing, too. Likely they heard me ask Mom what became of my p.j.'s.'

From the wall to the right a chuckling little-boy voice inquired, 'Well, what did become of 'em, kid?'

Sue flounced on her cot, making a face of violent protest, and the little boy snickered. Kim, from the corner which he had curtained with a sheet, made his voice deep and inquired, 'What's-this-what's-this, young people?'

Sue dozed at length, rousing with a start whenever a searchlight lashed in at the window. Toward morning her slumber deepened into profound sleep, so that when she wakened she pushed hard against the unfamiliar hammocky sag of her cot, refusing to open her eyes, though daylight shone through her lids.

The noise bewildered her: thudding feet, shrieking beds, slamming doors, crying of children. She could hear the clamor of birds, the rattle of palm leaves. She could smell spicy fragrances. Yes, but battling those aromas was the unmistakable edge of horse odor. And on Sue's nose a fly settled and bit viciously. Her eyes popped open and she stared up into the bare rafters, where more flies buzzed and circled. Her gaze flew to the windows, round the board walls. At a pushed-out knothole she caught the glint — the blue glint — of an eye. Jerking the sheet up to her chin she called indignantly, 'Kim! Look at that knothole!'

Before Kim could respond, the eye vanished, to the accompaniment of a loud smack and an aggrieved 'Ouch! I only wanted to see what the kids looked like.'

Sue leaped from bed, snatched an envelope out of her suitcase, licked the flap, whacked it on the wall so that it hung over the hole. 'My grief!' she protested.

So the first day began.

6

LIFE ON A RACE-TRACK

The first day began. A new life began; or a
strange section of life, how short or how long
the Oharas could not guess.

'It is like a summer camp,' Sue thought,
'only at most summer camps everybody is of
a kind. All high school or college girls, all boys,
all church people. And they are at a summer camp because they have chosen to be. Here we have no more
choice than a herd of animals, and here are every imagina-
ble kind and class of Japanese, and some that do not seem
Japanese at all. That blue eye at the knothole ——'

The blue eye sat one table away from the Oharas and
Itos at breakfast next morning.

'Look at him!' Sue exclaimed angrily to Tomi, next her
on the bench. 'Red hair. Nose like a scallop. And the
rest of the family — if they're Japanese, I'll eat my hat.
I haven't heard a single Japanese word from their stall,
either.'

'Name Tommy Filkins,' Jiro murmured across Tomi;
'age nine. Tribe looks like red Herefords in a bunch of
black Aberdeens.'

'They rest my eyes,' Sue admitted, in the undertone
they were all beginning to use when they wanted to say
anything confidential, indoors or out. 'I wondered if they
could be put here to spy. Doesn't seem possible, but
Tommy'd make a fine tool, the monkey. It's good to see
somebody cut by a different pattern, though. Did I tell
you the rhyme Ai's brother wrote to us, after they'd been
in camp a few days? "Japs to the right of us, Japs to the
left of us, Japs to the rear of us, Japs to the front of us; I

45

never saw so many Japs in my life." Well, neither did I.'

Then she looked at Tomi and burst out laughing. Tomi's pained, shocked face protested against Sue's taking on her lips the hated and poisonous nickname, 'Jap.'

'At least there's a variety of styles,' Sue went on, reverting to her earlier thoughts.

Jiro nodded. 'Next our stall, other side,' he said, 'the folks look like millionaires.'

'And beyond these Filkinses,' Kim chimed in from across the table, 'the toughest-looking gang!'

'Already I hear that they are Etas,' said Mrs. Ohara. In Japan the Etas were outcasts, and even in America their taint hung over them like a bad smell.

'Might turn out an experiment in democracy,' Jiro said. 'Everybody on one level, same food, same roofs ——'

Kim's face darkened. 'In a democracy every fellow's supposed to have a right to rise above the dead level. What chance is there here?'

'Well, Doctor Ishamoto is in camp. Organizing lecture courses in biology. And you two kids and Tomi get a chance to finish your high school and graduate.'

'Commencement behind barbed wire,' Kim muttered. 'Commencement in a vacuum.'

But with school assignments to fill and camp routine to learn, Santa Anita proved no vacuum.

It was full of all kinds of activity. At dawn next morning Sue, stirring sleepily on her narrow bed, heard wheels squeaking past, feet crunching. She ran to blink through the window. Women and girls were pulling toy wagons — mail-order wagons, she learned later — piled with bundles of clothing, soap, buckets.

Next day Sue and her mother joined that parade. They lugged their wash to the one big open laundry house and stood in line for their turn at a faucet. Before they could reach it, the clangor of the breakfast dishpan made them rush home with their clothes, rush on to join the breakfast queue. Next day they reached the wash-house at five-thirty.

As Sue sleepily blinked at the scene around her, she thought the early hour as nice as it was queer. Fenced-off grass and shrubbery sparkled with dew, and a gossamer thread spun from palm leaf to ground glinted in the early sun. In a tall poppy hedge a silken red bud split its green cap and opened before her eyes. 'It's funny how we waste gorgeousness unless something forces us to use it,' Sue told herself — 'go along, losing the loveliest things ——'

Sue's thoughts were pulled away from nature to human nature. Here was the woman who lived beyond the Itos, awkwardly washing out delicate bits of lingerie. Here was the peasant type from the stall beyond the Filkinses', clumping across the sloppy floor on getas, wringing heavy garments with accustomed hands. Here was a Doctor of Philosophy, small and merry-eyed, her head done up in a vari-colored silk scarf, and next Sue was Tommy Filkins's mother.

As she straightened her back and smacked a lock of flaming hair out of her blue eyes, she recognized Sue. 'Oh, you live next door,' she observed. 'I surely want to apologize for our Tommy.'

Sue stiffened. She had had to paste two more envelopes over Tommy's enterprising peepholes.

'He's always been a handful, Tommy has, but the weeks since we've been here he's really got out of control,' said Mrs. Filkins, vigorously sudsing a grimy pair of small shorts. 'There's no holding him, in a place like this, where he doesn't have to come home even when he's hungry. But his peeking at you like he does, that's just because he's so curious about the Japanese. We lived

ninety miles from the Coast, in a little town where there
wasn't a one.'

Sue blurted out, 'But if you aren't Japanese, why on
earth are you here?'

Mrs. Filkins scrubbed and talked. 'Everybody won-
ders. Well, this is the way of it: My husband's father
had a Japanese grandmother. Her husband — that's
Tommy's great-great-grandfather — was an English sailor,
and I guess it was a regular movie affair, and he married
her and fetched her to America.'

Sue stood gaping, a rope of soapy pink crêpe in her
hands. 'And you mean you aren't Japanese at all, yourself?'

'Not one speck. No, I'm Scotch-Irish-English-Dutch
— and all American. Dick's father and uncle and aunts
every last one married white folks, and so did their kids.
But just the same, Tommy's of "Japanese descent."'

'But surely you wouldn't have had to come here.'

'Tommy had to, and so did his dad. You wouldn't
expect me to just shuck them off, would you? All the
other husbands and wives felt the same way. Except
two.'

'There's another redhead eating at our mess hall,' Sue
said contemplatively.

Mrs. Filkins clucked as she threw a twist of nightgown
over her drenched shoulder. 'Mhm: Taro, the kid that
lives with a bunch of other orphans in the street back of
us. But if you look close you'll see his hair's black at the
roots. Poor fellow, he bleached it; bleached his skin, even
— and wore black goggles, hoping he could keep from being evacuated. But the F.B.I. isn't so easy to fool.'

Sue happened to sit in sight of the polychrome boy at
breakfast. Having risen so early and done her bit of washing and left her clothes stretched on the lines in the back

part of the wash-house, Sue felt righteous and very hungry. But in spite of appetite, she found her thoughts straying to this strange boy. He even ate unboyishly, without zest, and his pallid face was as opaque as a whit-ened window-pane. 'How scared he must have been,' Sue thought, 'or how deeply humiliated. It must be hard on him now, to be a figure of fun rather than of tragedy.'

'You go at your studying as soon as you've made the beds,' Mrs. Ohara said, when they came out into the early summer sun. 'I'd rather iron than not. I even wish there were dishes to wash. It's a queer world, without dishwashing.'

Was it only last December that Mother had said, 'It's a good thing there are always dishes to wash'?

Sue found it hard to settle down to schoolbooks. Kim already lay flat on his stomach on the asphalt floor, con-centrating on the pages under his nose and making an oc-casional lunge after a horsefly that circled his head. Kim had always been a student. An energetic brain made good grades easy for Sue, but study had never allured her, and only the fun of school competition had carried her high on the honor roll. Now she puttered around as long as she could, sweeping, hanging up clothes, hunting new peep-holes, before she perched on her cot with a book.

Next door Jiro was working busily on a wardrobe for the Ito stall. He had spent a few days making careful drawings, consulting the Oharas about them. He had chosen a modern style which depended for its effect on fine proportion and careful finish. Today he was begin-ning the work, and the clean smell of pine boards hid the odors of ammonia and horsehide.

At mid-morning Sue and Kim and Tomi left their books to go with Jiro to the scrap-lumber heap. Beyond hospital and fenced-in gardens, new barracks had been built to house another seven or eight thousand evacuees after the stables were filled, and the left-over wood was free for camp use. The young people soon found good pieces for Jiro's wardrobe doors, and then they went peering into the new barracks, still vacant.

'See, they are flimsier than our stalls,' said Sue.

'Our establishments have more stability,' Kim drawled.

Sue and Jiro laughed as if the joke were the funniest on record, and Sue's heart bounced up. Kim's black moods depressed her.

She picked up a small, smooth board and carried it home. There she knelt on the concrete and worked diligently with Jiro's thick carpenter's pencil. Presently she held up a sign, HOME OF WHIRLAWAY. From beyond the hallway and half-doors, Jiro's eyes hid themselves in his lashes, and he laid down his plane and took up a piece of board himself.

'My letters aren't so fancy,' he said presently. 'But how's this?'

His sign said, SEABISCUIT SLEPT HERE.

Tomi regarded it questioningly.

'Oh, gosh, kid! don't you ever read anything but the funnies? These are like the signs, "George Washington Once Slept Here," or "Bonaparte Ate Here." I'll nail 'em both up,' Jiro added.

Santa Anita broke out with a rash of street signs and placards: WILSHIRE BOULEVARD, HOLLYWOOD BOULEVARD, MAN–O'–WAR STREET, JERKS' JERNT, THE JIVE CATS. One of the new barracks had chalked on its window: NO JAPS NEED APPLY.

Some of the stall windows carried service flags with one star or more; some bore V's for Victory. One day the young people found a V with AXIS lettered after it.

'We — we ought to report it,' Sue stuttered furiously.

Kim went deep red, but he muttered defiantly, 'Well, maybe there isn't so much to choose.'

Sue gasped, and Jiro slapped Kim's shoulder and said, 'Shut up, fellow,' as one might say it to a sick child.

That night Jiro came in smiling so broadly that his eyes were furry slits with dancing lights shining through. 'I smeared their Axis for them,' he said, dusting chalk off his hands. 'And I made a swell cartoon of Tojo hanging by a noose from the V.'

'Strange there can be such zest behind the barbed wire,' Sue thought. 'But all the same,' she added, the words coming out without her meaning them to, 'I don't see how we're going to stand Easter.'

'Those good friends of yours, they forget Easter,' Tomi said disagreeably.

'Well, for cat's sake, Sis!' Jiro snapped at her.

'I suppose you expect them to carry us on their shoulders, Tomi,' Sue said. 'After all, they've got their own lives to live.'

Naturally Tomi would be a little jealous of the Oharas' many Caucasian friendships. But her words had brought Sue's hidden unhappiness into the open. The Friday before Easter, and not a word from Cordova all week. Was it true that these camps were tombs, and the Oharas a forgotten family?

7

VALLEY FORGE

Saturday morning. The day before Easter. Sue and Kim sat on the floor with their biology notebooks, inking in the drawings they had sketched at home in the Cordova lab. The only other place to work was the big room at the grandstand, but its tables were always crowded, its clamor deafening.

Tomi sat on a cot, sighing and turning the pages of a textbook. Mother had the electric iron attached to the light cord that swung from the rafters, and was pressing lengths of flowered scarlet calico. She had ripped up Sue's broomstick skirt to make appliquéd designs on unbleached muslin she had bought for curtains and bedspreads: already a community store was going full blast in camp. Jiro was sociably sandpapering his pine wardrobe, just beyond the half-door. The common wood, repeatedly rubbed down and shellacked, acquired a lovely glow, and even its brown streaks and knots became decorative. Beyond Jiro Sue could see his twelve-year-old sister Mitsu sitting in a corner with string stretched across her slender hands, making an intricate cat's-cradle for Kiku, who crouched between her knees.

'No, I don't see how we can stand Easter,' Sue said once more, and splashed a drop of ink on a carefully drawn cell.

Before the subject could be taken up again, Tommy Filkins stuck his head in the door. 'Callers for the 'Haras,' he announced, his blue eyes darting into every corner.

Sue jumped up, smoothing her hair with both hands

and leaving the blot to dry. Kim came to his feet as eagerly. Mrs. Ohara's fingers shook as she disconnected the iron.

'Couldn't be Dad,' Sue reminded her. 'Nor Tad nor Amy.'

Nevertheless, they walked so hurriedly across the camp that they arrived breathless at the rear entrance. Callers!

Many people clustered along the barbed wire, sitting or standing, talking across the prickly barrier. All on the inside were Japanese, but those on the outside were a mixed assemblage. There were Caucasians — evacuation had added this word to its everyday vocabulary — Negroes, Chinese, and even Japanese. For now, on April 24, evacuation was only half-completed.

Sue's eyes raced from group to group. 'Oh,' she cried, her voice catching, 'the Clemonses — and the Andrewses ——'

'And Jim Boyd, the nut,' Kim finished.

They clasped hands across the wire. Sue and Emily kissed. Everyone struggled for words and then talked all at once.

'We brought a cake — and cookies and junk ——'

'But some guy took 'em ——'

'Marian couldn't come. The Easter sales at the shop are marvelous ——'

'Almost everything you transplanted in our yard is growing like mad.'

'The kids in English class sent an Easter basket, but the guard took that, too. If they don't shell out, just let us know!' Jim flexed a threatening arm.

'We'll get the things,' they assured him. Of course they would. Everything was fine. Sue's face felt stretched with its smiles. This was next to being home again.

The young people dropped to the ground to talk more

comfortably, listening betweenwhiles to scraps of conversation from their elders on the one side, from a visiting
group on the other. The Clemonses could have come in
— ministers were allowed entrance; but they would stay
outside with the Andrewses today. Tomorrow they would
visit the Ohara stall, for tomorrow Mr. Clemons was to
have part in the Easter service. And now, what was there
that Mrs. Ohara would like him to bring her from town?

Some of the visitors on the other side were Chinese.
Even the old grandmother had come, in black coat and
trousers and with a funny black bandeau across the bald
spot on her brow. Evidently they were keeping their
Japanese friends' dog for them; the little black cocker
flew under the wire, long ears flapping, feet as big as if he
were wearing fur galoshes. He climbed into his young
master's arms, frantically licking the tears that ran down
the boy's face. Looking at him, Sue felt old and sad and
wise; and Emily reached through the fence and patted
her hand sympathetically.

Sue smiled at her and changed the subject: 'The
preacher's asking Mom what she wants. Know what I'd
like?'

Emily shook her gleaming head.

'A hamburger!' Sue gestured across the street.

Emily and Jim twisted to look. Directly opposite the
race-track entrance, beyond the highway with its stream
of traffic, stood a Drive-In stand.

'That's easy,' said Jim, on his feet with the words. 'I'll
be back in a smack with a sack.'

Sue put out a detaining hand. 'No, I didn't mean that.
I want to get it myself. I want to saunter in, free as air,
and sit down at the fountain like a princess, and eat two
hamburgers, with onions and dill and mustard and ketchup
and potato chips.'

Jim cast a quick look around him. 'That's easy, too. Look, kids, with all these other Japanese on the outside, how would anybody notice you weren't visitors, yourselves? All you have to do is roll under when the guards aren't looking.'

They gaped at him.

'Shucks, Kim, you roll under enough barbed wire when we go fishing,' Jim exclaimed. 'Just make sure there's no guard watching ——'

Kim's Adam's apple bobbed up and down above his plaid collar. Sue's head whirled. Emily babbled, 'Oh, do you *think* it's *safe* —?' even while she was grabbing the strand of wire and holding it high as Jim was doing.

They were wriggling under. They were sitting up, hearts pounding, outside the fence, furtively brushing dust from themselves. They were sauntering between Emily and Jim toward the strip of highway and its whizzing cars.

'Kimio! Sumiko!' Mrs. Ohara's shocked voice stabbed them. Two or three cars were roaring toward them, and Sue felt as if she were standing poised on the brink for minutes.

But she managed to turn and wave her hand, 'See you again soon, Mrs. Ohara!' she called. Her voice was strained and her body stiff from trying to be natural, and she could feel eyes boring into her from all directions.

'All clear!' Jim said, and they darted across.

By the time their first order was filled, Sue's heart had stopped shaking her. They ate two hamburgers apiece, though prices were outrageous; and they had doubledecker cones; and finally they sauntered back to camp, with cones for their elders held before them like flags of truce. They formed a knot before Mrs. Ohara, and by the time the cones had been distributed, Kim and Sue were inside the fence again.

'My grief!' Sue murmured, sitting up and brushing herself, while her stomach settled. 'I'd never have believed I could be so thankful to be on this side. Like a mouse safe in its own hole.'

Mrs. Ohara was scolding softly, and the faces of the adult visitors were variously amused, sympathetic, dubious, disapproving.

'Might — less innocent people,' Mr. Clemons wondered aloud, 'do the same thing — and keep going? Keep going?'

'There's roll-call, sir,' Kim put in quickly. 'Three times a day — and almost time for it now.'

So they said their good-byes, watched until their friends drove away, and loitered back toward their quarters. Later that night they investigated the gifts that had come from Cordova and passed inspection.

'I'm sure the cake is Mrs. Andrews's special chocolate angelfood,' Sue said devoutly. 'Emily put on the letters, though. Emily can't draw a straight line with a ruler.'

The inscription, HAPPY EASTER TO THE OHARAS, wavered in violet letters across the piled white frosting.

'Mrs. Andrews's own special icing,' Sue went on, running her tongue hungrily round her lips. Then she bent to look closer. 'Funny,' she said, 'I never saw any of her icing that was pockmarked like that — little bits of holes all over it.'

'They use long needles,' cheerfully observed Jiro, who had been invited in to share the goodies.

The others stared at him.

'You mean they — searched — our *cake?*' Kim asked.

'Now, Bud, be realistic,' Sue said soothingly. 'If any of the bunch is dangerous — and it's likely there've been dangerous ones, though most of them are in detention camps now — but if there's any chance, wouldn't the

Government be silly not to make sure no contraband is smuggled in? Though it does seem funny when they let us visit through the barbed wire.'

'Really dangerous guys wouldn't risk passing things in the open like that,' Jiro guessed. 'Or maybe the Intelligence is just getting into swing ——'

'Well, you needn't cut any of the old cake for me,' Kim growled. 'I've lost my appetite.'

Mrs. Ohara went on serenely, counting noses and taking expert measure of the tall cake, and then drawing a free-hand design of her own which made a many-petaled flower and reduced the confection to equal slices. And presently Kim was eating his share, with lemonade as cold as water from the tap two doors away would make it. The camp was soon to go on Army A rations, but as yet it was on B rations, and butterless, and meals were drab. The high, light cake, its delicate brown surmounted by drifted sweetness, was luscious after the dull tastes and textures with which their plates had been piled.

Easter eggs, both the genuine kind, dyed, and chocolate ones trimmed with crimped white sugar ribbons and flowing script, 'Love to Sue,' 'Kisses to Kim'; an Easter lily plant for Mother and an azalea for Sue, cookies, fudge, and panocha from the church choir.

'Maybe it isn't such a horrible Easter after all,' said Sue, when lights went out at ten and they groped their way to bed.

'As if a cake could make Easter!' Kim said loftily.

But for Sue the next day did make Easter.

The Oharas dressed carefully, glad that they had brought some good clothes, together with the work clothes mentioned in the instructions. When they came to the great grandstand it was evident that most of Santa Anita had done likewise. Thousands of people were assembled there, and they were as smart, as well-groomed, as any city church congregation.

The choir had been practicing under a noted Japanese director, and now the music swelled out gloriously on the soft spring air. Palms rustled, birds sang, the San Gabriel Mountains rose in beauty. Mr. Clemons offered prayer that was strong and tender, and the speaker of the day, a man known across the continent, lifted the hearts of the people.

As they walked home, Sue said haltingly, 'I don't know that I ever felt more Easterish.'

Even Kim's face was relaxed from its tight brooding. 'Remember it was just before Easter, two years ago, that I had my appendix out. That was the Easter that meant most to me. Up to now.'

Sue thought, 'It's the pain, the sorrow, that make Easter. There's no real Easter without the Cross.'

Kim's mind must have been working along like lines, for he said: 'I suppose good things are worth suffering for. I mean things like democracy. They don't come cheap. Maybe this —— You know what I want to name our stall? Know what I wish you'd letter over it, instead of your kiddish fooling? "Valley Forge."'

Sue's thoughts stumbled momentarily and then fell in step with his. 'Valley Forge,' she assented, *because all this would be dignified, made bearable, if we could remember to think of it so: as suffering for our country. For America.*

8

SOMEWHERE, SOMETIME

Sue's Easter mood of high joy faded, yet she found life unexpectedly normal after its violent uprooting. Much of the time it continued to seem like a big-scale summer camp. Father's absence did not destroy that illusion, for Father had always been too busy for vacations.

Except for missing home and family, his letters said over and over, *this idleness is the only real hardship. In good health. Plenty food, though hungry for my wife's cooking. No mistreatment, of course. If I could just know when I am to be released.*

Am fine, said Tad's letters. *Getting tough as nails. My only complaint is the difficulty of getting promotions because of being a 'colored man' in a white unit. They say some Japanese have been promoted, but I don't know of any. But the fellows are O.K. Do not be surprised if you do not hear from me for a while. Write as often as you can, and notice this new A.P.O. address.*

Written from a port of embarkation, Tad's words meant that he was soon to sail — somewhere, sometime.

Except Amy, everyone in the Ohara family was living on a somewhere, sometime schedule. Amy had an office job for the summer, and would be returning to Wellesley in the fall. She was treated well enough, she said. But she had found it good policy to dress in her Hawaiian costume and sing Hawaiian songs when there was opportunity. *Believe me,* she wrote, *the Hawaiian touch sure makes a difference.*

Sue answered that letter rather stiffly. Of course it was silly of her, but she felt as if her sister were not quite loyal. *I do think it's up to every nisei who's out from the barbed wire to be a committee of one to make friends for the whole bunch*, she wrote, *and not hide behind Mom's grass skirts*.

Sue usually made her letters as funny as she could, especially to her father. There was humor in Santa Anita, and laughter, even though the issei, trained to self-control, preserved blank faces. There were the mice that frisked through the bedrooms at night, and the robust flies which the Oharas had inherited from the previous tenants. There were the cartoons Jiro drew on the envelopes Sue continued to paste over knotholes Tommy Filkins continued to poke out. There was the comic-strip character, Li'l Neebo, created by an evacuee artist. It helped a lot to see that absurd, big-eared, cross-eyed little Nisei boy go through the experiences they were going through themselves.

Self-consciously Sue sandwiched Jiro in between mice and flies and Li'l Neebo. She didn't want him to stand out too boldly, yet she would have felt sneaky not to put him in at all, when he was the most important feature of Santa Anita. Of course Mother must be writing Father about the enforced neighborliness of the Oharas with the Itos; and Sue could imagine how surely she pointed out Jiro's crudities. Mother simply could not imagine that Sue was seriously interested in him — that was one safe-guard. But Sue's heart thumped every time a letter came from Father, for fear he had written, *about this Ito boy, Sue, I wish you to end the friendship at once*.

Further to keep Father's attention from the Itos, Sue wrote very dramatically about the sports program put on by Japanese-American Y workers, the basketball games which lasted till the lengthening shadows sent the young players dashing to the bath-house, only to find the showers closed. With only one bath-house for fifteen thousand people or more, showers must be shut off at eight to save water. Sue wrote, *Imagine us coated an inch deep with sweat and dust and having to stay that way. You never miss the water till it's turned off.*

Kim, who seldom complained of physical discomforts, wrote in on the margin, *It's like democracy; you don't appreciate it till you've lost it.*

In June the letters from Cordova were full of graduation, class day, parties. It gave Sue a strangely forlorn feeling to hear of all the gaiety and not be in the midst of it. *Her* best friend, *her* class, *her* club, *her* prom, for which Mother had already planned a 'gorgeous white formal' — and Sue shut away behind barbed wire.

She threw up her chin and filled her own letters with high-school commencement, too: Santa Anita commencement.

It was held on the great grandstand, at six-thirty in the evening. The orchestra played the 'Pilgrims' Chorus'; the stadium grew still; the mountains turned sapphire and rose in the level rays of the sun. Sue murmured, 'It couldn't have been half so pretty at home.'

Kim's expressionless eyes flicked toward her. She could not read them, these days, so rapid was the shift of his moods. Now, when the assemblage rustled and creaked to its feet to salute the flag, Kim brought his hand stiffly to his brow, but Sue saw with a sense of shock that he kept his lips firmly closed. Then in the midst of the pledge his voice rang out harshly, as if in defiance of an inner opposition: 'with liberty and justice for all' — and under his breath he added, with a corroding bitterness — 'all but us.'

'What is this doing to my brother and his hot young love for America?' Sue wondered. 'Why can't he take it like Jiro?'

Once Jiro said, interrupting Kim's passionate protests, 'You love your mother, even when she punishes you.'

'If she spanks you because you wear a yellow suit and some other kids in yellow suits bust a window?' Kim flashed.

Jiro's face had hardened with purpose. 'Even when it's like that,' he said.

Sue remembered that interchange now, as the concourse stood for the singing of the 'Star-Spangled Banner.' With the flag rippling against blue sky and violet and rose mountains, with the beat and clash of the orchestra and the soaring of multitudinous voices — 'O'er the land of the free and the home of the brave!' — the thought of Jiro's words made Sue's spine tingle. Another phrase recurred to her, out of Sunday School or worship services. How did it go? 'Though He slay me, yet will I trust in Him.'

'I'm all over goose-pimples,' she thought, 'like on Easter morning. Because, look, other people have suffered and died for their country, and some of them unjustly, like the Salem witches, and the Mormons —— And out of all the pain and the standing for what people believed has come this America. And it is still worth suffering for ——'

The speaker of the evening was introduced, head of one of the largest school systems in the world, and phrases of his address struck through the soft general stir, through Sue's millrace of thought: 'serving the country — the chances of war — possibilities for a new and better America — breaking down the little Tokyos and going out into the United States to become integral parts of it ——'

The mountains changed from one translucent color to another; the sky cooled; over to the westward hung the frail sickle of the young moon, the planet Venus a luminous miniature globe below. Sue, being Sue, noticed a clever twist in the glossy bob of the girl directly below her; new styles in the rainbow of dresses. She looked sidewise at Kim: his face darkened, brightened; his eyes burned and grew dull.

Why couldn't Kim —? Why couldn't Kim be someone else than Kim? He was made this way. He suffered. Like Taro, the boy three rows ahead, who had shaven his hair now, to get rid of the motley red; whose hands and face still held their unnatural pallor.

They suffered. They could not take this in their stride — 'and goodness knows it has to be a mighty long stride in any man's language' — take it on the chin, see fun where fun was, chances where chances were.

In one of his letters to Tad, Kim had written, *I don't mind about the inconveniences — and they sure make me sick when they gripe about these weeks without butter. No, physically we are getting no worse a dose than you and all the other soldiers. It's the mental agony* ——

Sue had always sparred with Tad; the two of them were on the bias, she used to say; but she liked what he wrote in reply: *Buck up, old boy. Remember there's lots of guys in this man's army that haven't come to camp because they wanted to, any more than you've gone to Santa Anita. They've had to give up their homes, too, and their schooling and their business prospects. They've had to leave wives and sweethearts. And their names aren't Watanabe or Miyamoto; they're Smith and Jones and Kelly. And remember, kid, democracy might have to use the tommy-gun of dictatorship to win this war, but if we don't win we might lose — everything. Freezing folks to their jobs isn't democratic, either, or a lot of the other things that have to be done now* ——

Kim had flung that letter angrily at Sue, exclaiming, 'It's different, and Tad knows it's different, unless he's

even dumber than I think he is. If it was the whole of
America that was being evacuated! But this is class discrimination ———'

Sue's mind came back for the speaker's concluding
words, and she rose with the rest of the graduates as they
were presented to their respective principals. A rush of
warm feeling flooded her at sight of Mr. Banning. He had
come all the way from Cordova to give three pupils their
diplomas. The rows ahead of her moved forward to re-
ceive the little squares of parchment, and presently she
and Kim and Tomi followed them, and stood before their
principal.

This was the peak of another hill, and perhaps peaks
always looked different when you reached them. This
was high-school commencement — commencement! But
where was Emily? Where Gloria and Jim and Elsa? And
how queer that all these hundreds of graduates should
have black hair and black eyes!

Mr. Banning halted the slow-moving line, a hand on
Kim's shoulder, a smile for Sue and Tomi. 'Tomorrow
night in Cordova I shall read your names,' he said: 'Tomi
Ito; Sumiko Ohara, salutatorian; Kimio Ohara, vale-
dictorian: in absentia; gone at the call of their country.'

There was an instant's hush, and then the grandstand
burst into applause, and the line moved on.

Receiving their diplomas, the graduates returned to
their seats and stood until the last boy and girl had
passed their principal. High on the grandstand a bugler
sounded taps and reveille. Sue did not look at her
brother, but she heard him sniff, and conquered the im-
pulse to slip her handkerchief into the clenched fist that
touched her powder-blue skirt. Wouldn't he be mad if
she did such a thing!

The last clear notes died on the air and the orchestra

struck into the Wagner chorus again. Boys and girls shuffled and clicked and clumped along the grandstand seats and gathered around the entrance, at the fountain, between the palm trees. They exchanged congratulations and jokes; they scribbled autographs on the mimeographed sheet headed SANTA ANITA COMMENCEMENT; they lingered till twilight had thickened to soft dark.

That night Jiro gave Sue and Kim a present. It was a double desk. No secrecy had been possible in its making, with every hammer blow audibly announcing it; but Sue had supposed that it was for his own family. She passed an admiring hand over its clear, glowing surfaces, its clever drawer-pulls. She stumbled in her thanks, for the gift had surprised her, and, besides, Mother was observing her with an expressive lack of expression.

'You'll have studying to do,' Jiro explained, 'and it's been sort of inconvenient ——' Jiro's russet face was flushed and his eyes sparkled.

'But what's the good studying?' Kim demanded. 'Because where do we go from here? And when?'

Jiro said: 'Yes, but pal —! Why not get the good out of the bad right now? Like Booker T. Washington calls them, the advantages of your disadvantages. He was a Negro. Compared to the Negro, we don't know what suffering is.'

'And where are those advantages?' Kim asked.

'For me,' said Jiro, 'this great biologist, lecturing on the grandstand. And a prof from medical school giving orientation lectures ——'

Couldn't Mother see what a real person Jiro was?

'Orientation?' Tomi stammered. 'Oriental?'

'Gosh, Tomi, what a little dumbbell!' Jiro spoke sharply and then twisted a lock of her hair with caressing roughness to make up for his disgust. 'It's finding out

what you want to do — when you can. I'm taking a job
as gardener, too.'

'For sixteen per month?' Kim inquired.

'Not so much less pay than a soldier, at that,' Jiro said.

9

MEMORY BOOKS AND ROMANCE

The next week life began to shift into new patterns.

Mr. Clemons had written about the Oharas
to the Japanese Baptist minister, and Mr.
Banning, the high-school principal, to some of
the directors. As a result, Sue found herself
enlisted as a teacher before her lofty enthusiasm had had
time to cool.

School was a necessity, to give the children constructive
activity. But among the Japanese-Americans there were
few trained teachers, because the profession was almost
closed to them. They could take all the education courses
the university offered, and be graduated with honors, yet
find themselves in a blind alley with their degrees and
their certificates. Teaching positions were only for the
noted like Doctor Terami, or like Doctor Ishamoto, who
had sat high on a university faculty: high and secure, until
evacuation brought him to camp as quickly as it had
brought the Itos from their farm and the Maramis from
the fish cannery on Terminal Island and the Watanabes
from their vegetable stand in a Hollywood market.

Now, for lack of trained teachers, college men and
women and high-school graduates were called to the task
of manning the Santa Anita school. Sue met with a

hundred others in the huge grandstand room and soon was feeling her way through kindergarten classes in the wake of a competent slim girl who had taught kindergarten in a San Francisco mission. It was a queer school. Classes huddled here and there around mess-hall tables in the huge open room. A class assembled before the windows marked 'Pari-Mutuel,' and others near windows marked 'Five Dollars to Win,' 'Ten Dollars to Win.' For this was where bets had been placed when Santa Anita housed race-horses instead of people.

Old men and women gathered for study round a mess table in one corner and, at another, women learned new crochet patterns. Sue raised her voice to say, 'Now, children, march round in a circle, and climb up on the benches at our table. Now, quietly! QUIETLY!' Tiptoeing with exaggerated care, she had to shout the 'Quietly!' to make it heard above the clamor. At the same moment the nearest teacher was saying, 'Watch the blackboard, boys and girls, and you will see how we prove the theorem that a straight line is the shortest distance ——' Her voice rose to a shriek, and Sue and Miss Saito flapped helpless hands and giggled, while the kindergarteners thumped down their sturdy little feet, surveying the distracting scene with absorbed interest. It was a strange new world for these babies, but not too strange, since their mothers were in it, and teachers, and other babies. Little shiny-eyed, shiny-haired dolls, they marched, sang, squatted, jumped, often a bit behindhand because they were watching the big boys and girls. And when Miss Saito devised a playhouse for them they forgot everything else and were on a happy island of their own. The playhouse was marvelous, with all sorts of readymade cubbyholes and cupboards, and others which needed only a board or two for completion.

Once, that first week, Sue stopped and laughed until she had to lean against the long counter that formed the front wall of the playhouse. A few children stopped their work to watch her and join uncomprehendingly in her laughter, and Miss Saito narrowed her long dark eyes in a sympathetic smile. 'But what's funnier than usual?' she asked.

Sue waved a limp hand. 'All of this,' she gasped. 'Kids learning their numbers around the betting windows, and that smell of fish soup and Japanese pickled radish floating out of the swank Santa Anita coffee shop. But the funniest of all is the babies playing house in the — in the bar!'

Out in the open grandstand gathered the junior high classes and the adult English students. And part of the stand was given over to a Government project, the making of camouflage nets for the war. Strange, over against the heterogeneous school, those huge nets hanging free from the rafters. Workers, men, women, girls, stood along the ascending aisles and in front where a few seats had been removed for the purpose. Their hands were busy at the new craft, and their faces were hidden by masks, for protection from the flying lint.

None of the Oharas and Itos worked on the nets, but most of them were busy. Mrs. Ito was studying English, which she had never mastered because she had hardly needed it. Mrs. Ohara took wood-carving. Jiro attended evening lecture courses under his learned scientist and physician. Kim sprawled on his cot, reading books and magazines from the miscellaneous Santa Anita library. And Sue sat in on the World Literature lectures.

'I think maybe what's happening to me is that I'm growing up,' Sue said wonderingly to Jiro as they sauntered home from their grandstand classes one evening.

The fragrances of summer were in their nostrils, the stars bright and close in their eyes; and a great pink moon was caught in the fronds of a palm tree. 'Yes, I do believe I'm growing up.'

'Good!' said Jiro, adding hastily, 'But how do you mean?'

'Well, I really get a thrill out of learning how to manage those blessed little monkeys — almost as much as out of a dance or a basketball game. And here's what's funny: I enjoy Doctor Noda's lectures. I'm not listening just to get an A in an exam. Why didn't I ever guess that literature was like that?'

'Mark Hopkins on the other end of your log,' said Jiro.

Sue looked at him cloudily. Funny how Jiro, with half her opportunities — and words — seemed to have so much more intimate an acquaintance with the world of thought. 'You'll have to make me a road map of that remark,' she said.

Jiro laughed. 'Me and my quotes. Know where I get 'em? *Reader's Digest*. Well, somebody said, quote, A liberal education is Mark Hopkins on one end of a log and the student on the other. Unquote. That's not exact. But it seems that Mark was some great teacher.'

'Doctor Noda on one seat in the grandstand and Sue on another,' Sue translated. 'Next you'll say these swell teachers are an advantage of our disadvantages. All the same, I'd manage to get along without them if I could be outside this barbed wire. This horrible barbed-wire fence.'

After the one madcap expedition for hamburgers, Sue had not stepped outside. First, because Mrs. Ohara forbade; second, because it was impossible. No longer were there Japanese among the visitors; all the West Coast Japanese were in this camp and others. Only a few seriously ill in hospitals and a few orphans in institutions were left outside in this 'vital military area' one hundred miles deep. And, lastly, the visiting arrangements had been changed, and a visiting room had been provided near the gates. Here callers sat on one side of a table and hosts on the other — a table too broad to touch hands across.

So the barbed wire became a symbol; that and the searchlight. Sometimes even Sue lay sleepless, watching the lights pass and pass again, and wondering whether some poor human being, trying to escape the camp, might be caught under the merciless glare like a little wild creature flattened against the ground, eyes bright, heart pounding — some boy, perhaps, like Taro, who had disfigured himself because barbed wire and searchlights were so hideous to him ——

Once in a while it gets you down, she wrote to Emily. *Barbed wire; flashlights; you get to wondering if Japanese blood really may be criminal, to have to be shut up and hunted down like this. Then Jiro Ito says, 'Quote. Noda stands forever as one of the great medical explorers, living and dying for the good of mankind. Unquote. Quote. Many Christian thinkers regard Kagawa as one of the three greatest spiritual leaders now living. Unquote.' Jiro is wonderful.*

Mostly, the Santa Anitans were happy, except the Kims and the Taros, and the artists and business men and professional men who had been so engrossed in their work that it was pain to leave it. Even Mother said it was rather fun to have no dishes to wash for a while, and no food to cook — or it would be, she always added, if Father were with them and they knew that Tad was safe, and if they had any idea how long this was to last and what was to come after it.

It isn't quite living, Sue wrote Emily, *not to know what*

*will happen from month to month.   Not to have any notion
when nor where nor how.*

Toward the end of July, people commenced learning
some of the whens and wheres.   Numbers were posted:
families from, say, 100 to 140 and 4001 to 4270, would be
sent to Colorado River Relocation Center on August 26
and August 27.   Each time the *Pacemaker* published a
new set of numbers, Sue's eyes tore through the list in
frantic haste.   Where would the Oharas be sent?   *And
where the Itos?*   To a California camp?   To Oregon, Utah,
Arkansas, Arizona, Colorado — all strange and barbaric
sounding to their provincial ears?

Now, strangely enough, Sue found herself clutching at
the things that were Santa Anita, tasting the loveliness of
its setting, laughing at its great, clamorous schoolroom,
savoring experiences like her occasional meal with other
teachers at the Red Mess Hall rather than at her own.
The Red Mess Hall was in the grandstand instead of in
the barracks.   Its ceiling was high, so that it was not so
stifling hot; its tile floor was colorful; those were the only
differences, but they were noticeable ones.

And at Music Appreciation hours, on the grandstand
at twilight, Sue tried to fill her eyes and ears full, as Miss
Miyamoto played fine phonograph records, lent by
evacuees all over camp, and gave brief talks about them,
while sunset transfigured sky and mountains.

'After all,' Sue said one night as she and Jiro and Tomi
walked home, 'this might be one of life's great adventures.
I want a scrapbook, so I won't forget little things.'

Jiro made the scrapbook.   In its pine cover, rubbed
satin-smooth, it had a knothole; and on the first page Jiro
drew a cartoon of Tommy Filkins, to grin through the
hole.

Sue was surprised by the number of mementoes she

had accumulated, beginning with the leaflet dated April 2, 1942, and titled:

INSTRUCTIONS

to all persons of

JAPANESE

Ancestry

Civilian Exclusion Order.

There was her tag, like a baggage check: SUMIKO OHARA, 5463–B. *You are instructed to report ready to travel in own car, 8:30, Morning, April —*. There was the instruction sheet handed her mother on entering camp. There were copies of *Pacemaker*, with Li'l Neebo's engaging grin; and bulletins of church services; and the multigraphed program of the high-school commencement.

There were the first letters to come from Father, with the censor's red stamp in the corner. There were favors from a Y.W.C.A. party, and a program for the Southern Jamboree, where they sang Southern songs and Sue was one of a dozen Daisy Maes and Jiro one of five Li'l Abners. There were newspaper stars colored blue and red with crayons to decorate the hall for a Fourth-of-July party. There were drawings by Sue's kindergarteners.

'When we leave here, I'll put in my mess-hall button,' Sue said. 'It's certainly a vital part of camp.'

'No button, no chow,' Jiro agreed.

Jiro, Tomi, Sue, and Kim had gathered in the Ohara stall, as they so often did in the evening. They had pulled the desk over under the electric bulb, and Mother had her folding chair beside it, to catch all the light she could. Sue had spread her souvenirs and the new scrapbook over both halves of the desk, and Kim retreated before the flood.

'I can't see why you want to perpetuate this nightmare,' he growled, stamping across the room. 'Hugging your chains!'

Mrs. Ohara's gaze followed him anxiously through the door. Santa Anita had its gangs: a few genuine American gangsters done in yellow, and a few young amateurs who called themselves Yellow-Shirts. 'Kimio is too fine to be tainted,' Mrs. Ohara had repeatedly assured Sue. Yet she was happier when he stayed at home, though his gloom darkened the room.

'He thinks his number's a disgrace,' Sue said soberly, when her brother had gone. 'But as long as there's no striped suit attached, I'm going to make mine a talisman: 5463–B. Look, it's two nines, five and four, six and three; and I always was partial to nine. If only I'd thought of this book earlier: there are a lot of things I wish I'd kept, and plenty I wish I could have.'

'What?' Jiro asked, fingering her mementoes.

'Well, those first newspaper accounts of the evacuation. Why on earth didn't I keep them? And if we were only allowed to take pictures: snaps of our stall, and of the track ——'

'Wait a second!' Jiro bade her, striding across to the Ito stall.

Sue was uncomfortably aware of her mother's glance. 'Passed in front of me without asking pardon,' it said. 'No manners, daughter!' Sue dropped her eyes to her book and busied herself pasting in an invitation to a Girl Reserve party.

Jiro came back with a handful of clippings and a pencil drawing of the movie theater across from the front entrance. It was labeled, INSIDE LOOKING OUT.

Though hampered by ordinary pencil and tablet paper, Jiro's long, square-tipped fingers had again proved their skill.

She said, 'Jiro, you ought to be an artist.'

Jiro replied: 'With a surgeon's instruments, I hope. Sue, I'll try any sketches you want. Of course they aren't snaps, but they might do. And you can have the clippings.'

'But then you wouldn't have them.'

Jiro looked at her. Mrs. Ohara's brows shot up, and her cool face was forbidding.

August passed. All the Poston contingent were gone. The Santa Anita stores exhausted their supply of hastily ordered autograph albums and sent for more. The next groups were sent to Heart Mountain, in Wyoming, and many of their number bought denim overalls and checked shirts and bandannas from the mail-order houses.

'Since we've got to go somewhere,' Kim said, 'I wish it could have been the Wild West.'

Sue felt her stomach churning with a constant unrest. The family's summons came early in September. At the last of the month families 5200 to 5463 would be moved to Amache, Colorado; and, two days later, families 5464 to 5700.

Sue and Tomi had held their breath as they read the announcement. They dropped the *Pacemaker* and stared at each other. As if intentionally, the numbers had divided their families from each other.

'My grief! Like when the teacher separated Em and me in study-hall!' Sue went off like a firecracker. 'Oh, Tomi, it would have been such fun to travel together.'

'I knew something bad would come,' Tomi mourned.

'Well, for Pete's sake don't act as if it were forever,'

Sue scolded. 'What's a couple of days? At least you have Jiro to make it interesting.'

'Jiro won't put himself out for only a sister like he does it for you!' Tomi retorted with a flash of spirit. Then she shook her head timorously. 'But my father has ask to be send to Topaz camp, in Utah, where is his brother.'

Sue's spirits dropped.

Now preparations crowded the days, and leave-takings. Wood was given the evacuees, to box any furniture they had made in camp, and there was a constant racket of sawing and hammering by day. The evenings were kept for good-byes, and the night before the Oharas were to be moved, a party at the grandstand entrance bade farewell to the young people about to go.

'Let's take a last look across the barbed wire at that theater,' Jiro proposed suddenly, as the phonograph stopped and all the dancing couples dropped limp from each other's hands. 'Won't you, Sumiko?'

Sue hesitated. Mother wouldn't approve. But goodness knows Sue and Jiro would be well chaperoned. Never a minute, anywhere in camp, that everyone wasn't chaperoned.

'Well,' she assented. 'It's been the Promised Land all these months, hasn't it? But it's not your last look.'

'Isn't it?' asked Jiro.

'I wish we could stay in California,' she said hastily, as they strolled toward the entrance.

'California doesn't want us.'

'But I want California,' she said stubbornly.

If she had been Kim, she would have flung her arms wide, to take it all to her heart: sparkling night sky; slender palm bolls; grotesque palm crowns far overhead; roses breathing perfume through the dark; mockingbird, voice of California, scattering mellow notes in his sleep.

'It was only the pressure groups that didn't want us,'
Sue argued. 'Because of our farming more scientifically
and living on less, so they think we take jobs away and
bring wages down.'

'Yes,' Jiro agreed, 'I got hold of a Congressional report.
On evacuation. Shows how unfriendliness to Japanese
was worked up on purpose. Far back as the early nineteen
hundreds. Even says Hawaiian planters stirred up the
Americans. So we'd have to quit coming to the Mainland.
Then they thought we'd come to the Islands instead.
They needed us that bad.'

'I'd rather it would be business and politics than —
than folks,' said Sue.

'The way this report had it, not many folks wanted us
all evacuated,' Jiro said. 'Only those that were scared
by yellow newspapers and magazines. I like California,
too. Who doesn't? But, Sue, we don't know any other
section. Perhaps we'll get to like the rest of the country.
Utah — lots of history in Utah. Did you read "Children
of God," in *Reader's Digest?* All about how the Mormons
came to Salt Lake?'

'Surely there isn't much chance of your going to Topaz?'
Sue tried to make her tone indifferent.

'My father has asked for the change.'

'They say it's fearfully hot and fearfully cold at some of
these camp sites,' Sue said forlornly. 'And they have
thunderstorms. I never did see a hard thunderstorm.
And in Arizona the camps are on Indian reservations,
aren't they?'

Jiro nodded. 'Funny if they kept us on reservations
for good, like some of the Indian tribes,' he suggested,
picking up a stick and twanging the barbed wire.

'My grief!' Sue ejaculated, looking across at the neon
signs and at the stream of headlight stars that flowed

between theater and Santa Anita gate. 'Right now I can't think of anything but being free of this barbed wire, though. Imagine being outside again. What else matters?'

Camp lights and headlights showed Jiro's face intent upon her. 'Something else matters to me,' he said, his voice so sober that Sue looked away uneasily. 'Did you know the boy beyond Filkinses marries the girl next door to him tonight?' Jiro asked abruptly. 'Scared of being separated. Lots of couples are marrying for that reason.'

'I'd hate it,' Sue expostulated. 'Think of starting your married life where twenty people could hear every time you said "dear" — could almost hear if you *thought* it! You'd never catch me marrying in this Union Depot.'

'Waste of time to talk to you about it, then,' Jiro said gravely.

'Why, I'm only eighteen,' Sue stuttered. 'And, besides, Father and Mother would never let me ——'

'Would never let you marry an Ito?' he asked. In his jeans trousers and plaid shirt he stood solid and strong, head thrown back, looking thoughtfully out across the highway. 'And you so modern. Now I never used to worry when my folks talked of employing go-betweens to find me a wife ——'

'Really?' Sue felt herself flushing, though she should not have been shocked. Even here, wedding notices in the *Pacemaker* often said, 'Baishakurin were Mr. and Mrs. So-and-So and Mr. and Mrs. Such-and-Such.'

'Well, you know my folks. And those marriages seem as successful as others. Besides, since I knew that my father wasn't likely to approve of the girl I'd always dreamed about —— But now I plan the American way. Even if I have to wait till I'm an M.D. and my girl's got her first gray hairs ——'

Jiro was turning the matter off lightly, yet not without making his intentions clear. His thick eyelashes laughed at Sue, and the corner of his mouth quirked up, but she couldn't laugh back. She was cross: cross with her parents for feeling superior to the Itos, cross with the Itos for daring to disapprove of the Oharas, still crosser with them for daring to think of marrying Jiro off. *What kind of girl would they have chosen?* Cross with Jiro, she couldn't explain why. With all this boiling emotion, Sue was glad when the lights of Santa Anita went off with a snap.

'Ten o'clock? The heck it is!' Jiro brought his watch close to his eyes to make sure. 'We better run.'

Sue was already running, and Jiro loped easily at her side. 'Good night!' she said breathlessly at the dark stall door.

'And I don't care if it's good-bye,' she thought irritably, clicking the door shut behind her.

10

OUT FROM THE BARBED WIRE?

In spite of Sue's rebellion, there was pain in her good-byes next day.

Jiro acted as if he had forgotten the evening before. His manner was brotherly as he helped the Oharas, carrying Mrs. Ohara's bags and Sue's over to the fenced enclosure where the travelers were assembling.

'You make a swell redcap,' said Kim.

'Dime a dozen,' said Jiro. 'Breakage guaranteed.'

Crowds waited outside the enclosure, to bid farewell to the departing. For the Oharas there were Tomi and

Mitsu and Kiku, Miss Saito and a girl Sue had grown
fond of. There was a boy in the coveralls of the Santa
Anita fire department. There were Mrs. Filkins and
Tommy, and a few flip youths bantering with Kim. The
youths Mrs. Ohara regarded with distaste, suspecting
them of being Yellow-Shirts, and with relief because they
were booked for other camps and Kim would no longer
associate with them.

There were tragic faces in the crowd. Violently pushed
into intimacy, these people were now as violently torn
apart. To be reunited when? Ever?

Sue watched a slip of a girl who had always reminded
her of the butterfly dancer in her doll collection: so lithe,
so finely fashioned, so long of eye and tiny of mouth.
That slip of a girl shook with silent sobs as she said good-
bye to a shock-headed, russet-faced boy. The boy was
headed for an Arkansas camp; and the girl's parents were
engaging matchmakers to arrange a suitable marriage for
her after she reached the Colorado center. The shock-
headed boy was not suitable.

The young fireman fished a carved wooden object from
his coverall pocket and handed it across to Sue. 'To remember me by,' he said soberly. 'I tried to make it look
like you, but it isn't so hot.'

'Then it would be to remember *me* by,' objected Sue,
'and I only need a mirror for that. Thanks, Tim,' she
said, holding back a giggle as she pinned the gargoyle face
to her lapel. Glaring eyes and Medusa locks were pains-
takingly inked into the pine.

'Well, look here,' grumbled Jiro, setting down the bags
in his hands and shifting the other two from under his
arms to the ground. He also fished a carving from a
pocket, and presented it, with a mock bow from the hips,
like the ceremonious salute of the older Japanese.

'Oh — lovely!' Sue cried, inspecting the spirited little horse. 'It's Seabiscuit, isn't it?'

'Yes, I copied it from the statue, sort of.' His look added, *But to you and me it means Santa Anita. And the circle around it means, who knows when and where?* 'And there's your lucky number, Sue: 5463–B.'

'Would you please pin it on for me?' Sue asked.

The young fireman watched somberly, and Mrs. Ohara tilted a critical head at her daughter as Jiro pinned Seabiscuit to Sue's remaining lapel.

'You better shove those bags under so the inspectors can inspect,' Mrs. Filkins said, observing the young people with indulgent amusement.

And Tommy Filkins said, 'Hey, you'll miss me something awful, won't you?'

The bang of inspected suitcases speeded up, and the scrape and shuffle of baggage and feet across the floor. It was nearly train time. A public health doctor and two nurses who were assigned to this movement came hurrying out. The first travelers filed through the visitors' room to the entrance, checked and counted as they went.

The butterfly girl put on a piteous smile and the shock-headed boy folded arms across sweatered chest and stared away from her. 'They act as if they were the only ones,' Sue thought. 'If it were I, I would not let anyone see how I felt. No, I shall be as gay as if the parting didn't hurt at all.'

At this point Kiku threw back his head and howled, and Sue was suddenly glad to drop on her knees and reach through the wire to him and let her tight-held face twist up without anyone's wondering why.

'You're — going — back to America!' he gasped between desperate sobs. 'I — want to — go back with you.'

Kim said roughly, 'We're not going back to America,

kid, not by a long shot. And is there an America, anyway?'

'We've got one more stopover,' Sue told the child.
'Just one more stopover, honey man. And even that'll
be outside the barbed wire,' she added vehemently, getting
to her feet as Jiro swung the little boy up on his shoulder.

It was time for the Oharas to shove on through the
visitors' room to the long train puffing and snorting on the
tracks behind the stables. And then, heads out of windows up and down the train's length; hands waving to
Santa Anita and hands waving from Santa Anita; smiles;
wet lashes; stolid faces and desperate faces and hopeful
faces and careless faces.

And good-bye, Santa Anita, dissolving already like
colored clouds at sunset. Race-track; mushroom city of
eighteen thousand people of Japanese descent; army
camp to be.

What next?

That day passed swiftly. There was the train to ex-
plore, coach after coach of black hair and black eyes, with
no Caucasians except the trainmen and the doctor, nurses
and M.P.'s, who stayed mostly in their Pullman. Two
other Pullmans were filled with mothers and babies, the
old and the sick. Each coach had its monitor, to keep
order and to get off at stations and buy needed articles:
soda pop, bananas, aspirin.

'You'd be a good monitor,' an official had said to Kim
when appointments were being made. 'Fellow like you,
with brains and background — man, he can go anywhere.'

Kim had scowled pointedly toward the barbed wire.

'Ohara,' the young official said patiently, 'be realistic!
Let's make the most of what we've got. And try to please
people. It's biting off our own noses, not to try.'

'That's easy,' Kim had muttered, 'for you, a Caucasian.

Not for me. If I scowl, they say, "Look at the Jap, mad
at being given a soft living, when his own country's freezing prisoners' feet off and starving them to death." And
if I smile, they say, "See the insolent, sneering Jap."
And if I try to hide my feelings, they say, "There's no
safety with folks that can hide their thoughts like that.'"

Kim was not made monitor, and perhaps he wished he
had been, now that his mood was pleasanter. With so
much to see, he was like his old self.

There were plenty of children to keep the train lively.
In the seat ahead of Sue was one of her favorites, seven-
year-old Mary Kaneko. Mary began the journey gazing
sedately out of the window. Soon she was on her knees,
peering around the seat at Sue, then on her toes talking to
her across the top, and finally squeezed in beside her,
playing out-of-the-window games. 'Who'll see the first
cat?' Sue said, as they pulled into a town. 'Who'll see the
first cow?' as they drew out into open country, seared
brown now by the long dry season.

Mary was as tiny as the average four-year-old, with
bones so small and fine that knees and elbows and wrists
showed themselves only as dimples in satiny skin. Satin,
or fine china, thought Sue, cupping a hand over a delicate
knee, free from flaw and immaculate as if soil could not
cling there.

Mr. Kaneko turned and asked, 'Our little daughter is
not annoying you?' He spoke politely, but as if it were
unthinkable that Mary could be anything but a privilege.
Sue shook her head and hugged the child, carefully, not
to rumple the small smocked dress which also was crisp
and smooth as porcelain. Yet Sue was glad when Mary
sagged with sleep and went to curl up for a nap between
her father and mother.

Sue was glad to be free because now there was still more

to see. The young Oharas had never passed the borders of
California. When they drew out of San Bernardino —
little San Berdoo — leaving it behind them, white amid its
palms and roses and oranges, they were venturing into new
territory. They climbed the steeps of Cajon Pass. They
gazed at the jagged naked peaks and at small mining towns
running up their sides and perching on the slag heaps, and
at great white hills like embankments of metallic snow,
which had something to do, Mr. Kaneko explained, with
the extraction of gold by cyanide.

Mr. Kaneko had been a professor in one of the Coast
universities, and he knew everything. And Mrs. Kaneko's
family had grown wealthy in some learned profession or
other. The fine worsted of Mr. Kaneko's suit and the
sleek simplicity of Mrs. Kaneko's showed wealth as
plainly as their speech and manner showed breeding.
Sue wondered whether they had ever ridden a day coach
before, or eaten from paper plates in the diner. It was
not regular diner fare, they commented to the Oharas,
looking companionably across the aisle at them as they
ate, but it was very good. It was almost a religion with
them, as with Mrs. Ohara, Sue thought, not to express
discomfort or dissatisfaction. They could not have been
more nonchalant if they had spent their lives being shut-
tled around from old stables to rude camps in hot, dusty
old troop trains. But the food did seem marvelous after
the months of Santa Anita fare, and everyone ate with
relish.

Presently the train was running through the Mojave
Desert, and all up and down the coach faces were pressed
to window-panes, staring at the endless wastes, the great
cacti, the Joshua trees like rheumatic giants carrying
petrified feather dusters. At a small station, a green
oasis in the burning expanse, where the evacuee train

drew to a siding to await the passing of a troop train, the
evacuees were allowed to get out and stretch their legs.
Sue had thought that any kind of fresh air would be better than the hot stuffiness of the train; but the desert heat
struck her like a blow in the face and seemed to blister
her lungs as she breathed it. She was not sorry when the
awaited train had whizzed past, khaki heads and shoulders
at every window.

Night fell, lights were dimmed, and the travelers dis-
posed themselves to sleep. Folded papers rustled, as
people tried to cool themselves. There were the crying
of babies, an occasional cough, a wide variety of snores.
Sue was delighted to find that the aristocratic Mrs. Kaneko
snored, though she had to admit that it was a well-bred
snore, a soft soprano that broke off now and then as if the
sleeper disciplined herself even in sleep. And then Sue
also slept, and wakened only when too loud a silence dis-
turbed her and she guessed that their train had pulled to
a siding and was waiting for some regularly scheduled
train to pass it.

Evacuee trains could not upset the complex network
of travel, so the trip was prolonged by interminable waits.
Next evening found them still far from their goal; and it
was that evening, in their brightly lighted little world
flying across unknown night, that they met sinister adventure.

'Cowboys!' exclaimed Kim, as they stopped for orders
in a small station. 'Gosh, they might be bandits.'

All the young in the coach surged to that side and flattened eager faces against the windows, gazing at the
mounted men whose horses tossed impatient heads just
outside the circle of the station lights. The nisei were
film fans and knew their cowboys.

Then came the sound Sue could not soon forget: an

unfamiliar whine, and the crash of glass. Little Mary shrieked, and Sue stared from the splintered glass in her lap to the men outside. There were muffled shouts, and the train jerked into motion before the horsemen had wheeled away from the track. One looked back over his shoulder, and the light streaming from the windows gave Sue a snapshot of his face, all malevolence and triumph.

The monitor called out to the people to lower their shades. Some remained up because no one dared stretch out an arm. The monitor darted along the aisle, jerking them down.

Mr. Kaneko, grim-faced, dabbed at Mary's cheek with cotton from a first-aid kit Mrs. Kaneko held out to him. 'It was only a fragment of glass,' he assured her, 'not a bullet. You'll be all right, darling. You'll be all right.'

Mary choked back her sobs and her arms loosed their strangling clutch of her father's neck. She pushed back to peer into his eyes, her own face, the red wound sharpening its pallor, grown suddenly old. 'Daddy,' she faltered, 'those men — Daddy, aren't we really people?'

Kim said bitterly to Sue, 'The answer is No. And you better stick a piece of that glass in your Memory Book.'

Sue could think of no effective reply. Mary's question had moved her more deeply than the attack — which had strangely enough wounded no one but Mary. And now the tight-closed train, fleeing, secret and hunted, through the hostile land, gave her a sick sense of apprehension.

But she squared her shoulders. 'These drawn shades make it stuffy,' she said stoutly.

M.P.'s strode through the train, speaking with bluff sympathy. 'Better hurry through the vestibules if you must go to other coaches,' they warned. 'And let the monitors do the shopping ——'

The nurses, coming through with salt pills to combat

the oppressive heat, were refreshingly indignant. Their shocked exclamations when they saw little Mary's face were balm to Sue.

With the morning, when shades could be snapped up again, life looked more bearable. Such an attack was not likely to be repeated. Then, too, the train was passing through Indian country, and the nisei were keenly interested in Indians. They were allowed to get off at a small station, and here they found Indian women sitting on the platform amidst displays of pottery, and Indian men hung with belts, blankets, and beads like walking curio shops. Here, too, the heat had moderated. Life was in the air, and hope.

Among Arizona's cliffs and buttes of sandstone, brickred and chrome-yellow and cream, streaked in with shadows of purple and red crayon — among these dramatic rock shapes, the young Oharas first saw the bowl-shaped huts of the Navajos.

'Look, Sis,' said Kim, 'the girl herding that flock of sheep! She's wearing a dress like those in the movies. I always thought they were faked.'

Mrs. Ohara gazed from behind her smooth, emotionless face, all the while doubtless thinking anxiously of Father, and whether he was getting the right food for his sensitive stomach. Sue pressed her face to the glass and said, '·There's one just Kiku's size. He even looks like Kiku.'

They passed other Indian homes, dust-colored houses almost invisible against the rocks where they perched.

'If only Tomi were here to enjoy it with us, this would be really fun,' Sue declared, dividing her attention between the window and the handkerchief doll she was making for Mary.

'Tomi!' jeered Kim from the seat behind.

'Quite likely the Itos will go to Topaz,' Mrs. Ohara

observed frostily. 'You may have to get used to doing without them.'

'Nobody but Mr. Ito wants to go there,' Sue stuttered, her head bent above the handkerchief toy. 'But of course he's the one that counts, in their old-fashioned ideas.'

'Jiro's the only one that's got out from under his thumb,' Kim agreed. 'I suppose Jiro'd be saying this was one of the advantages of our disadvantages. We're getting to see America. But I prefer to go under my own power, thanks.'

A passing boy stopped and slapped Kim's shoulder. 'You and me too,' he said. 'This business of being herded like cattle! It shows how much democracy's worth, when it can haul off and paste its citizens like this.'

Sue whirled to see how Kim would take the criticism. He looked flushed and uncertain. 'It's a wartime measure, Ike,' he mumbled. 'A democracy can't function so democratically when it's got a war on its hands. And it's for our safety, too. If folks feel like that about us ——' He gestured toward one of the broken windows, patched with adhesive, 'and you have to admit the authorities are decent. Look at the food we've had on this trip ——'

'Aw, come off! Didn't you hear of the bunch who didn't get a bite to eat for a day and a night, kids and old folks and all?' This boy, Sue thought, looked like the cartoons labeled 'Jap' in the newspapers.

Kim bristled. 'You have to be fair. You know darn well everybody runs into things like that now, with the troops exhausting the supplies. You don't need to be a sap.'

'And you don't need to be a sucker,' Ike sneered. 'I thought you were the fellow who didn't swallow all their lies. Likely you're satisfied with the J.A.C.L., too, and the way they've let us down. Wish I knew what they got paid for giving up after they'd promised to keep us from being robbed of all our property.'

Kim muttered, 'Maybe they had to give in to save bloodshed.'

'Oh, yeah? Well, which is better, bloodshed or the kind of treatment we're getting?'

He thrust a newspaper under Kim's nose. Sue could read headlines: 'JAPS CODDLED AT AMACHE IS CHARGE'; and smaller print: 'Luxury food to Japs while Americans starve.'

'Booting us out of our homes and grudging us grub and a roof! The heck with America!' Ike shrilled.

Kim let go with his balled fist, and the two hurtled into the aisle, clinching and growling like fighting dogs till the monitor hustled up, ordering anxiously, 'Stop it, fellows! Break it up!'

The journey was one of those endless ones which does, unbelievably, end at last. Tracing the course by a railway folder, Kim at last announced that the next station was Lamar, Colorado.

'And Granada just beyond — and Amache!' Sue responded, reaching up to the luggage rack for her hat.

The feminine Oharas put on hats, coats, gloves, sat forward in their seats. Kim dragged down the bags. The train pulled into the small city of Lamar and puffed and jerked and let off steam interminably, while a freight clanked past. As soon as they had pulled away from the brick-paved tracks, Sue and Kim crowded toward the rear door of the coach, luggage in hands.

They seemed to creep onward for a half-hour before they came to the still smaller town of Granada, where they clambered out, hearts crowding into their throats.

Townspeople loitered along the streets or lined up against the little yellow station, or leaned over their fences, watching. Mary Kaneko buried her face against her father's arm. *Aren't we really people?* With an ache for the sensitive child, Sue thought, 'They do look at us as if we were animals being herded into the zoo.'

A car stopped on the highway, and from the driver's seat a man's voice bawled, 'There you are, kiddies. You always wanted to see some live Japs. There's a whole mess of 'em.'

Sue thrust out a defiant chin and looked away from the sightseers. Deliberately she studied her surroundings. The cottonwood trees of the village were turning gold with late September. The houses were drab and low, the town flat, as if a roller had passed over it. Beyond it lay farmland. Amache stood in the fertile Arkansas River valley. Now the valley was brown and yellow — stubble-fields and long lines of yellowing cottonwoods.

Sue looked at her fellow travelers. It was true that they did not resemble an American group. The issei, Japan-born, were generally under height, short of leg, large of head. They huddled together, bowed by the weight of their luggage, or cowered above it where they had set it on the ground. Their faces were blank. The blankness of despair? Of stoicism? Of indifference? Sue shivered. She was glad when she and hers could climb into the trucks that had come for them and be on their way to shelter.

The trucks started up a dun rise of ground from the village, and Sue pointed a shaking finger. There rose an encampment of long buildings, all alike. Above them, a giant on stilts, straddled an orange-and-black water tank.

'I don't know but this is the worst moment of all; it's so ugly, so dull, so dry.' Sue swallowed as if her throat were parched. California might burn in the dry season, but all around her Sue had been used to year-long green-

ery. Here was no green, and the lack of it seemed to sear
her lips, to sear herself.

'It is like an army camp,' she said gamely. 'And no
barbed wire.'

It was Kim's turn to level a finger. The truck was
turning in at the entrance of Amache and passing the
sentry-box. A half-mile to the east, a half-mile to the
west from the camp gate, out toward watch-towers that
reared their heads above the rolling ground, stretched still
the hated strands of barbed wire.

11

TAKING IT ON THE CHIN

The truck rumbled on into the encampment inside the barbed wire. It rumbled past a barrack where Old Glory flew high and a khaki-clad
soldier did sentry-go, back and forth as if
worked by machinery. It passed barracks
labeled Office, Reception, Fire Department.
It rumbled upgrade toward scores of others, set square
with the world and each other.

A gust of wind picked up the ground and filled the air
with it. The breeze stiffened till the dun oblongs of the
buildings were veiled by the swirling sand.

'There come the inmates,' Kim said, peering, 'to welcome the new prisoners.'

'Hush!' Sue hissed, feeling grim herself. 'This is going
to be our home for a while. Let's take it on the chin.'

Hunching their sweaters over their heads they stumbled
out of the truck, eyes blinking and teeth gritting on sand.
Men and women, boys and girls, crowded forward, search-

ing for faces they knew. The younger ones shouted greetings and the little ones peered from behind their mothers. Old inhabitants, in Amache two days or a week, maybe, pointed out the mess hall where the new ones were to go for induction. Assignments were quickly made, and the Oharas came out into the whirling dust again, and followed the pointing hands of the oldtimers. Into 4F — 10–A they ran breathless, and the wind jerked the door from Sue's hand and slammed it shut behind them. They were at home.

Home was a room sixteen feet by twenty-four, its walls paneled by two-by-fours, its floor of bricks laid directly on the ground. It held three cots, cousins of the Santa Anita cots, three mattresses, six blankets. A light bulb dangled in the middle, and at one end stood a fat G.I. stove and an open wardrobe. The thin walls shook, the windows whistled thinly between their teeth, the bulb swung on its wire.

'Come on in, Mr. Wind,' Sue invited, jocularly.

The sand did come in. The Oharas smelled and tasted it. It lay underfoot. It curtained the bare windows.

Someone rapped. 'Supper's at five-thirty,' said the boy from next door. 'In the block mess hall. I'll show you where.'

'Is there a place to wash?' Mrs. Ohara asked, looking at her grimy hands.

'Won't do much good,' the boy answered cheerfully. 'Bath-house, far side of this block — I'll show you.'

His matter-of-fact friendliness made them all feel better, even while buffeting their way against the blowing sand which made the short walk long. There was water in plenty, the boy said, pointing to the seventy-foot tank. They could bathe any time of day, and, believe him, they needed to.

Mrs. Ohara and Sue went in at the women's door of the bath-house.

'Very neat,' said Mother, looking around at the unfinished gray concrete and the white porcelain.

'But — my grief! no doors to anything,' said Sue.

The mess hall resembled those at Santa Anita: a barrack filled with long, low tables, and with kitchen fittings fenced in by counters at one end. The Oharas took the plates that were handed them across the counter, filed to a table, climbed over a bench and sat down.

'Gosh,' said Kim, 'this feels like children's furniture.'

'"All Japanese are short of stature,"' their guide quoted, grinning. 'They built these tables correspondingly.'

In every group there were a few issei who fitted the low furniture as a child fits its desk.

At each place stood a thick cup and an apple, and along the table at intervals sliced loaves of bread. Women brought pitchers of hot tea and filled the cups. The tea felt good to Sue's sandy mouth, but her head whirled from the journey and she was glad when her mother rose to go.

'You can take your dessert along,' the boy said, pocketing his apple and leading the way to the shelf where they scraped and piled their dishes.

When they got back to their barrack, they found their baggage-car luggage already inspected and deposited there. Each Ohara, being over sixteen, had been allowed to bring a hundred pounds on the train with him. Mother and Sue made the beds while Kim built a light wood fire in the army stove, and then they perched on their cots, with magazines on their knees for desks, and wrote their first letters from Amache.

'If you get near enough the fire so your fingers aren't too stiff to hold the pencil, you're too far from the light to see what you're writing,' Sue complained.

'Quit crabbing,' Kim mumbled. 'Do you have to wiggle so? Your cot rocks my cot and I don't know how you expect me to write straight.'

There's one thing you've got to say for old Kim, Sue wrote to Emily: *he doesn't gripe about physical discomforts. Unless, of course, it's his sister that's to blame for them. I try to keep thinking, myself, This is being a Pilgrim; this is being a pioneer; this is helping to make America. I won't go on record about Amache tonight, though. Mother says it will look better tomorrow, because 'night and tired-outness never tell the truth.' But though Amy's often talked about bare trees and brown grass, I never dreamed how it would be. To have everything drab, even the air, with the sand in it, why, it's like a dead world. No green; no fragrance; and, Em, so far, no mockingbirds. The only birds I've heard have been magpies, chattering like fussy old folks. Excuse pencil. My pen's empty, and we have to wait till tomorrow to get ink.*

In bed that night Sue lay awhile with her hands under her head. The wind had died down at sunset, and through the small high windows shone the stars, even brighter than in California. To the south, peeping over a roof, was the crooked W of Cassiopeia, which she used to see from her four-poster at home. Father had first showed it to her, together with the Great Dipper and the Swan, and had told her the Japanese stories that his father had told him about them. Sue would not let the tears come. That day when they had buried Skippy and their childhood, she had finished with tears.

Kim gave her the relief of laughter. From his sagging cot he snickered, '"Japs At Amache Coddled!"'

'My bed's sort of a hammock,' she responded.

'Mine's a celery dish,' he said. 'Pretty swank.'

Next morning Amache looked no better to Sue. Not only was she dizzy and nauseated, but her heart beat

quick and light and her ears rang as if they were under
water.

'You look as yellow as a Jap,' her brother taunted her,
after breakfast.

'The cup of coffee was good,' Mrs. Ohara observed
practically. 'Coffee; and an egg ——'

'But, oh, for one slice of your toast, hot and buttered,'
Sue moaned softly. 'Or a waffle and puffy brown sausages.
Kim, did you ever dream how delicious a slice of hot toast
could be — buttered?'

'You give me a pain,' Kim said. 'And you know what
the papers would say, "Compare that food, and this camp,
with what the prisoners get in Japan and the Philippines."
Of course the argument is fooey: those are prisoners, and
we're not. We're evacuees, moved-outers. And that's
totalitarian, anti-Christian Japan, and we're America,
fighting for democracy and religion. Anyone's just not a
real American who thinks we ought to come down to
Japan's level. But all the same there's no percentage in
belly-aching over hot toast.'

Today Kim seemed less depressed than Sue.

But it was a bad day. There was no discounting the
fact that it was a bad day.

'And now, again, no dishes to wash,' Mrs. Ohara said,
finishing the beds and sitting on one with slim hands
folded. 'You talk of toast. I should be satisfied with a
dishpan of hot suds.' She shivered in the sharp drafts.
'And a clean dish-towel and all the breakfast dishes to
wash: our own dishes.'

Throughout the early morning Sue also shivered in the
clear, bright chill. Kim built another small fire, but the
camp had been warned that the stoves must be used
cautiously until they had been more fully safeguarded.
Fire was an ever-present danger.

'I'm going to press some clothes,' Sue said, pulling her cot under the light cord and climbing up to unscrew the bulb.

'Careful!' Mother cautioned.

The cot lurched, bucked like a swaybacked broncho, and pitched Sue to the brick floor with a loud explosion.

'I always wondered if light bulbs really went off like that,' Kim said interestedly, when he had helped her up and found that the broken glass had not cut her.

'My grief!' she protested. 'Well, hold the darn thing, can't you?' and she stubbornly jumped up again and screwed in the iron-cord, while Kim braced the wavering bed and Mrs. Ohara held the iron.

Sue jumped down, grabbed a board from the top of their bedding box, thumped down a folded blanket and a sheet on it, and a magazine for an iron-stand. 'People are too easily stopped by trifles,' she said complacently, testing the iron with a damp finger.

She looked up in alarm: crackling blue sparks flew out around the electric connection.

'You blew a fuse,' Kim said, with a smirk. 'But you won't be easily stopped by having the whole barrack mad at you.'

'So ironing's out,' Sue said disgustedly. 'So what is there to do till our desk and table come from Santa Anita?'

Mother motioned meaningly at floor and windows. 'We can scrub,' she said.

Kim was prodded into buying a broom, a mop and soap at the Co-op. Mother and Sue carried water from the wash-house. The three washed the windows and scrubbed the floor. By noon, when the sun had climbed high and Sue's blood began to flow again and her fingers to lose their purple, the wind sprang up, flung sand on the shining panes, sifted it on the damp bricks as a huge sugar-shaker might shake sugar.

'My grief!' Sue exclaimed, clasping her ringing, dizzy head, 'I quit right here.'

'We'll put up our Santa Anita curtains and hide the glass,' Mrs. Ohara said practically. 'And we could get bed-lamp frames from the mail-order, and cover them with muslin with calico ruffles. I suppose we can get a three-way plug and have a light for Kim's bed also. A bed-lamp is comforting.'

Sue flung herself across a cot and moaned: 'A three-way plug would blow out fuses. And how you can think of such frivolous matters, Mother! Doesn't your head feel like a boiled potato? I wish I hadn't eaten the bologna. Our cooks seem very fond of bologna. And why do they boil turnips and carrots together for twenty-four hours or until thin enough to run through a sieve?'

Her mother swept the floor again, brushing up the doughnuts of fresh sand which industrious ants kept bringing up between the bricks. Groaning, Sue got up and took the broom from her mother's hands.

'Should your father come home unexpectedly,' said Mrs. Ohara, 'we would wish this place to welcome him. We must make curtains for the wardrobe. And why not partitions?'

'If only Jiro was here,' Kim said hardily, against his mother's slight frown. 'Jiro had some ideas about mov-able screens with translucent covering. I sure hope their old man didn't get his way about being changed to Topaz.'

Sue snapped, 'There comes the darned old wind again,' and kicked the wall. 'The day grows worse and worse, and so does this prison camp,' she thought, shaken with misery. 'Why, why, *why?*' she broke out. 'How did we ever deserve it?'

'A good part of the world could be saying the same thing today,' Kim stated, as if he were a lecturing professor. 'Ask yourself whether Japanese soldiers would have behaved as our M.P.'s did when'they moved us.'

'Do you think the stories are true?' Sue challenged him. 'About the dreadful things the Japanese do? You remember what Father said: that atrocity stories were sometimes manufactured. To build up hate. German atrocities in that other World War, Japanese in this. Because people seem to have to hate in order to fight and buy bonds.'

Kim contemplated his sandy fingernails. 'Some may be exaggerated,' he said. 'But Shig Nakamoto's brother has been a soldier in China, a U.S. Marine. And Shig has told me things I wouldn't repeat to you and Mother.'

Sue shivered.

Mrs. Ohara took the broom out of her hands and gave her a gentle push toward the door. 'Walk around and see who is here. See what this camp is like. Maybe not so dreadful.'

The wind was once more quiet, and the sand had settled innocently to earth, as if it meant to stay. 'But Amache looks as bad as ever,' Sue said, when they had gained its highest point. 'The better you can see it, the worse.'

'This is where the high school's going to be,' said Kim.

'How do you know so much?'

'Shig. The guy who showed us around. Not a bad guy. From Merced.'

Merced was the Center where most of the Northern California farmers had been assembled.

'This camp comes mostly from Merced and Santa Anita,' Kim continued. 'Farmers and fruit-growers, professional men and shopkeepers. You know the last movement from Santa Anita ought to come in tonight: it was supposed to start two days after ours. What do you bet the Itos aren't in it?'

'Oh, isn't this the most desolate place?' Sue gritted out the words as if they were an answer. 'I think the sameness of it will drive me mad. Twenty — thirty blocks all alike. All oblong, no-color barracks, twelve to the block, six apartments to the barrack. Two hundred and fifty human beings boxed in each one — like sardines ——'

'We'd be kind of glad if Tad was safe back in a camp like this, in good old U.S.A.,' Kim said gently.

But the bleak sameness whirled before Sue's eyes and she said despondently, 'This hasn't helped a bit, and I'm shakier and light-headeder than ever. Mother'd say it was unwomanly to whimper. But I want to whimper, and I'm going to.'

The day held two bright spots. First was Choyo Mori. Sue dragged unwilling feet to the mess hall and set down her filled plate beside Kim's. She glared at her heap of rice and at the lettuce leaf with a dab of jellied salad reclining feebly upon it. She glared at the waiting apple. 'An apple and an orange, an apple and an orange,' she thought unthankfully. 'Could anything be colder comfort for dessert? Or harder to eat decorously in public?'

Someone was plumping down on the other side of her, and Sue turned unexpectant eyes and looked into a face that made her own curve upward against its will.

'Hello, there,' the girl said. 'I'm Choyo Mori.'

Choyo wasn't pretty: body too small for head, mouth too large for face. Yet that mouth stretched up and out with a contagious gaiety; and the eyes were the candidest, kindliest, merriest ones Sue had seen in months. In spite of her persistent nausea, Sue had to respond to Choyo's gay stream of chatter; and when Mother piled her dishes and led the way primly toward the rear of the mess hall, Sue was surprised to find that she had almost emptied her plate.

'Tomorrow,' Choyo said as they parted at the Ohara door, 'everything will be different. It was for me.'

Sue was shaking her head doubtfully as she went into the apartment. Why should tomorrow be different? Unless the new arrivals ——

Mother and Kim were home ahead of her, and other voices were mingled with theirs: a deep, sonorous voice and lighter, younger ones. A man, a boy, a girl turned toward Sue as she stood in the door: a Caucasian man, boy, and girl.

'My daughter, Sumiko,' Mother introduced her. 'Sumiko, Mr. Clemons wrote to the minister at Lamar, Mr. —?'

'Thomas,' said the stranger, engulfing Sue's hand in a big warm clasp. 'So you're Sue. Brother Clemons certainly sang Sue's praises. And Kim's. These are my young sprigs, Clara and Johnnie.'

They shook hands, and Kim pulled his cot up facing another under the light bulb, and they sat down.

'Mother couldn't come tonight,' Mr. Thomas rumbled. 'But she sent her regards and some fresh cookies. Yes, she sent her regards and some cookies.'

Mr. Thomas had the old-fashioned ministerial air, and the old-fashioned ministerial manner of repeating himself roundly, as if his mind had gone wandering off and left his mouth to carry on by itself. Sue and Emily had often poked quiet fun at Mr. Clemons for the same trick. 'But never again,' Sue vowed, 'never again. How kind his eyes are! And his handshake: strong and warm. As if we were human and mattered.'

'Mrs. Thomas wants you should come in to Lamar and have supper with us some night soon,' he went on.

Sue looked startled. 'Supper? Outside camp?'

'I believe they give a pass to Lamar once a week —

or maybe once a month, if you're above reproach. Shopping — womenfolks always have shopping. Always have shopping.'

Yes, how warm and comfortable that absent repetition. And to go outside the barbed wire — to go into a regular store, full of plain Americans, and buy something, it didn't matter what. Maybe Choyo could go along, and Shig, and they could perch on tall stools in front of a soda fountain, or sit in booths where people wouldn't stare. Or how wonderful if Tomi and Jiro —— But, no, Sue was building walls against the time when the last Santa Anitans should come and not any — not any Tomi.

'Next week!' chorused the Thomases, when the visit was over and they rose from the wabbling couches.

When the callers had gone, Sue said cheerfully: 'Why don't we get a basin and pitcher and keep water here in the wardrobe? It would seem quite homey not to have to walk a block to wash your hands. I believe I'd like one cooky·to go to bed on. My stomach isn't so much like a top spinning.'

She ate two cookies, and Kim three, and Mother nibbled one, delicately. 'Made with pineapple,' she observed, savoring a morsel. 'Maybe Mrs. Thomas would give me the recipe when — if we go to dinner there.'

Kim hooted. 'Where'd you bake 'em? On the electric light bulb?'

'We shan't be here forever.'

'Says you.' Sue reverted to melancholy and flopped over on her stomach, which was spinning again. One tomorrow after another stretched ahead, all alike, all coated with sand, and only now and then brightened by a warm Thomas handclasp or a gay Choyo grin, or by a soda in a real drugstore outside the barbed wire. 'Tomorrow — and tomorrow — and tomorrow.'

And then tomorrow was upon her, and it was brand-new. She blinked her eyes and experimentally opened and closed her mouth. Her ears felt better.

'What on earth are you making faces about?' Kim demanded, peering over his sheet partition.

'What on earth are you rubbering for?' Sue retorted. 'Get back into your kennel and let me dress. I'm starved.'

'Well, thank Betsy you're over your grouch,' Kim commented, disappearing. 'You are, aren't you?'

'What grouch?' Sue inquired, jerking on her clothes. 'Hey! I'm not wabbly this morning. Why's that?'

Coffee, egg, strip of bacon, had more flavor than yesterday's. Even the cold slice of butterless bread vanished rapidly. Choyo came in as the Oharas went out. 'Good grief!' said Sue. 'Is this what you meant, Choyo? Everything sort of sparkles. And look at the sky! Come over today, won't you?'

'It was altitude, partly,' said Choyo. 'First it makes you feel awful, and then it makes you feel grand. Some quicker, some slower. Sure, I'll be over.'

'Look!' called Kim. 'Sue, there come the trucks from Granada. Might be the last bunch of Santa Anitans.'

The covered trucks lumbered slowly up, and Sue ran toward the road, Kim loping after her. The trucks halted and Sue tried to hurry, her feet sinking deep in the sand, her heart thudding. People began to clamber out.

'Hi!' yelled Kim, 'it's Santa Anita all right. Look! Jim Ish!'

The newcomers huddled there, queerly foreign in the mass, like the group two days before at Granada station.

'Poor guys, they look done in,' said Kim.

'They were on a siding in Granada all night,' someone put in.

'They'll be fine in a day or two!' Sue sang.

Sue herself felt wonderful. She drew a deep breath of the pure, bright air. 'It is blue air, bright blue,' she thought. The road gleamed shell-white under the high blue arch of sky. Sue came up on her tiptoes. She felt as if she might be growing wings — as if barbed wire for once hardly mattered.

'Gosh, there's Tomi!' Kim said.

'Yes, I saw him!' Sue exulted.

Kim did not notice. 'And old Jiro! He sure looks fit. He sees me, Sue. Look at the grin on him.'

12

PIONEER AMACHE

Life at Amache set in with a rush. Raw new town of barracks, springing from amid the sagebrush, cactus, prairie-dogs and rattlesnakes. Equipment unfinished. Sand driving through the air.

Grumblers, of course. Resentful faces, of course. But busy people, too. Stoic faces. Unconquerably cheerful faces. And some of the young enthusiasm of a pioneer community.

The administration offices, down near the gates, were gathering a staff of Japanese, with Caucasian department heads. There typewriters clicked, telephones shrilled; and at noon and at half-past four chattering youths and girls trooped out and up the white road to the dun-brown barracks that crowned the hill.

Even Kim, lifted out of his dark moods, applied for a job of surveying, together with Shig. Jiro started at once as a hospital orderly.

'The Caucasian head is a good physician, and the Japanese doctors under him are the best. It may help me along,' he said. 'I think Tomi's dumb not to take training as a nurse aide.'

'My father say, no, I need not,' Tomi murmured, her broad face closed to the enthusiasm of her companions. 'If this country take me from my home, it can feed me. I need not work.'

'But wouldn't you *rather?*' Sue protested. 'I like to be doing something. And it's exciting to help start a whole school system out of a few boxes and some string!'

Sue had registered for nursery school teaching in the barracks set aside for classrooms.

'The barracks will do,' said the supervisor, Mrs. Fennell. 'Except for the tiny entrances and high windows.'

Sue knew that Mrs. Fennell was thinking what would happen if fire broke out. Sue could picture babies trying to reach those windows, four feet from the floor, their panes not more than a foot square; could see the little things massed and struggling at the single outer door ——

'I hope they'll get up the new school buildings quick,' she said with a shiver.

But Mrs. Fennell shook her handsome gray head. 'People are raising a racket about them,' she said anxiously. 'The bids are outrageously high.'

'Well, our children were taken away from good schools,' Sue reasoned.

Mrs. Fennell slapped paste on the neck of a life-sized pony she had cut out of wall-board; slapped on a crêpe-paper mane. 'I know they were,' she agreed. 'I don't have to be convinced. But some Colorado folks say, dozens of our own schools have been closed a year or two now, for lack of funds. They argue, why should Japanese children have so much spent on them when American youngsters are doing without.'

'*American!*' Sue protested.

Mrs. Fennell sighed. 'See the big box of materials the Denver churches sent us?' she asked, more cheerfully. 'Paper, scissors, sewing-cards. Something to start with. And the kindergarten tables and chairs have come from one of the Assembly Centers. The chairs are almost more than the babies can handle: made of scrap lumber. They'll do till the administration can get us better ones. Will you rule these big box-tops for attendance charts, Sue? Reminds me of my grandma, teaching in a little red schoolhouse.'

Sue thought, 'She's high-altitude, like Colorado. She walks with her head up, and her nose is tilted just enough to laugh along with her blue eyes. And even though her hair was cut by a smart stylist, it's breezy and boyish and just fits her. I'm lucky to work with her.'

All the departments spent long hours planning courses of study suited to the scanty supply of books, getting tables and bookshelves made from waste lumber, putting through requisitions for the minimum of equipment. The principals and most of the teachers worked with the zest of pioneers, drawn to the task by their interest in the difficult experiment and in the chance to build from the ground up. If there were a few who had come because the salaries were good, and without any real concern for the uprooted children and young people, their number was comparatively small.

The Home Economics Department at once projected a model home, to show how boxes, barrels, excelsior, scrap lumber, and paint could be used to make the barracks livable. The first experiment was a cornice board across the barnlike little windows, hung at intervals with two-toned percale curtains, so that two or more windows became a single gracefully long one. Next was a chair of pine planks, padded with excelsior, covered, skirted, and cushioned with chintz.

The young Oharas and Itos paused to peer through the window of the model home on their way to church one Sunday.

'Kim wants real partitions,' Sue said. 'Jiro, have you dreamed up anything that will give privacy without shutting off the light?'

'Yes, and sent for it. Viofilm. Used for henhouses.'

Sue grimaced. 'That doesn't sound inspiring.'

'May not sound, but it's going to look. What are you and Kim planning first?'

Sue tossed back her heavy hair impatiently. 'Everybody so busy fixing things up — it makes Amache seem too permanent. I don't like anything that suggests our staying, not even the ball team's calling itself the Amache Indians. Indians! As if we were on the reservation for good. No, I'd rather go on camping. No matter how hard we work at it, we can't make these barracks nice or comfortable.'

'Oh, but —— Why, some of the folks didn't have so good houses at home, even. And if they make these so beautiful like they show us how ——' Tomi stopped, flushing.

Sue understood. The Ito farmhouse had been less homelike than the Ito stall at Santa Anita. Jiro had had time to beautify the stall; on the farm he had been too busy for indoor work.

Probably a third of the evacuees were better fed and sheltered than before. Another third felt little change in physical comfort. To the rest evacuation had meant a plunge from gracious living to bare, unlovely existence.

The young people went on to Sperry Hall, the big central hall where the nisei held their services. As the barracks had filled and the population climbed to seven or eight thousand, the Protestant church membership reached eight or nine hundred, the Buddhist group a slightly larger number, the Catholic about seventy, with evacuee ministers of many denominations and faiths. The majority of the issei were middle-aged or elderly, and preferred to hold separate meetings in their block recreation halls nearer home, leaving Sperry for the English-speaking congregation.

This morning the big barnlike building was crowded, every chair taken. The four hundred young people rose and sang, sat and listened, and Sue kept wondering what it was about them that nudged her mind as if wanting to tell her something significant.

She wondered even while she listened to the sermon. Mr. Suzuki's ideas pricked her mind like cockleburs, and would not let her retreat into her thoughts. She liked to watch him, too, forceful and forthright, and looking more American than Japanese, even to the silver feathers in his black hair.

American! That was it, Sue thought, as the four hundred young people rose to sing 'My Father's World.' How many times, in the old lost years, Sue had sung those words in youth conferences, at Y gatherings at Carmel, at Asilomar. And these young people were like those young people, not like the beaten, baffled crowd of short-statured 'foreigners' at the station. These were of nearly average height, and, away from the restraint of the issei, they were nonchalant in bearing, open of countenance.

'The thing is,' Sue exulted, 'these are Americans, inside and out.' And her spirits surged up with joy and triumph at the discovery.

As they filed out at the close of the service, they paused to read the bulletins of the week's activities, chalked on the big blackboard. Movies. Ball games. Discussion group, debating — Was Evacuation Constitutional?

'Gosh,' Jiro protested, 'they may word it differently, but they always discuss the same thing. It's done. Why not talk about Where Do We Go From Here?'

Sue shook her head, blinking against the wind that buffeted them when they stepped out on the sandy path. 'I think it's a good thing to pull it out into the open. Doesn't it work off some of the poison?'

'Especially with Mr. John leading the discussion,' said Kim, walking backward in front of them with his collar up around his ears and hands deep in pockets.

Mr. John, like some others of the staff, gave evenings as well as days to the nisei. A portly young high-school teacher, Mr. John had ruddy cheeks and a rosy mouth that usually gripped a pipestem, yellow hair that was always tumbled, and blue eyes that were always sleepy. He was an astonishment to his pupils, for he used an unorthodox amount of slang, addressed them with elaborate sarcasm when they were annoying, and had a way of swinging himself lightly to the top of a bookcase and conducting classes from that height.

'Mr. John is sort of fascinating,' Sue admitted, nodding to friends on this side and that as they made their way through the crowd to the mess hall. 'Only he's so much like a large peach.'

'He's swell,' Kim said indignantly. 'He makes you feel human again. He suggested my taking this surveying job, and I'm sure glad he did.'

They worked along the line to the mess-hall counter, climbed over the benches and sat down with their plates.

'Yesterday we went out across the fields,' Kim said, between zestful sips of fish soup. 'It's land the Government has bought for the Amache farms, but it felt as if we were really free. And there was so much that was different. Those big domed magpie nests in the cottonwoods down along the streams. And when the wind came up through the scrub-oak it sounded like the ocean. Just now the milkweed pods are opening and spilling out that shiny floss. Don't you girls want some for fancy-work? Or how about minnows for kindergarten, Susie? I found a bunch in a cove, and I could take along a bucket to-morrow.'

He did not take along a bucket next morning, for a heavy autumn snow gave the surveying gang a day off. The storm caused wild excitement among the Californians. Many of the children were as much amazed as Kiku Ito, who looked incredulously at the feathery white masses and demanded, 'Well, who done that?' The children could hardly wait to test the new element, and mothers who had the necessary money hurried to the Co-op and bought snow-suits and mittens, while the young people made flat sleds from scrap lumber and coasted, shrieking, down the gentle incline from the crest of the camp. The school block was a mad flurry of flying snow and excited shouts.

After school hours, Sue and Kim took advantage of Kim's holiday to get passes and ride in to Lamar on the mail truck.

Lamar has lots of trees and bushes, Sue wrote to Emily that night, *and when they're covered with snow, and the wires and fences, too, they make you think of a poem by Whittier or somebody. The air's lovely after the storm, washed clean and starched till it crackles. The flakes are really tiny stars, like the pictures; but did you realize that they're wet? You ask if we don't want skis, in this 'mountain country.' Em, right here the mountains are so flat they're hollow. And Colorado people can say all they please about dry cold not being cold; something certainly reaches in through these single walls and nips your fingers and toes. It'll be better when they get wall-board on the inside of our barracks. They're beginning to.*

Sue wrote nothing more about the trip to Lamar, but there was more.

'I'm honestly excited,' she chattered to Kim as they picked their way along the slushy sidewalk and approached a store with the big sign DRUGS above it. 'Excited over sitting in a drugstore again and sipping soda through a straw.'

Just a nice little American town, she was thinking happily, sitting muffled up in snow and smiling as she and Kim walked through it. And she and Kim just an American boy and girl like anybody else ——

Kim's hand jerked her to a halt.

'What's up?' she demanded.

'Use your eyes!'

In the window, propped against bottles of hair tonic and flanked by a teddy bear and a casserole, a black-lettered placard warned, NO JAPS WANTED HERE.

Brother and sister plodded silently back to the parked truck, their eyes on the snow, already an ugly brown in the streets. Sue buttoned her coat higher as they waited: it was growing colder.

'The General,' a smiling little evacuee who helped with the mail, came out of a store, his long cotton work coat flapping, his arms piled high with bundles. He tilted his head back to grin at the young people over his load. 'Ice-cream soda taste very fine?' he asked, nodding cheerfully.

'No Japs wanted there,' Kim answered.

The General clucked and shook his head. 'But there are other drugstores more polite.'

'Sodas don't exactly appeal to me now,' Sue said.

13

THE WOUND

Under the bright October sun the snow disappeared as quickly as it had come. Kim went back to work, but rather sullenly. NO JAPS WANTED HERE. It had been a little thing, amidst the turbulence of the past months, but even Sue had been depressed by it. Was it a forecast? Would they ever be wanted? Anywhere?

When Mr. Thomas, the Lamar minister, came out to camp a few days later and asked the Oharas to Sunday dinner and church, Kim excused himself. He had an engagement with Shig.

'I don't feel up to going to Lamar again for a while,' he told his mother, after the minister had gone.

Sue wrote to Emily, *It was swell to be in somebody's home again, and the home cooking was sooper-dooper. Hot cornbread with butter; sugar and cream in our coffee; chicken!*

And in church there was again the feeling of being sheltered from the cutting wind. Yet even in the church, along with many hearty handshakes, Sue felt critical glances, and sensed the stiff, self-conscious backs of young Clara and John, who sat on each side of her.

It was as if they were daring anyone to be mean, Sue went on in her letter to Emily. *It's the hardest thing to let go and be natural when suspicious eyes are watching you. My grief, I've learned that!*

I was actually glad to get back to camp. It feels more and more like a world in itself, and I'm almost scared to have it that way. Yet we have to make it decent for the little children and the old folks.

While we've been waiting for more equipment, we've been

110

getting the children to pick up stones and outline a walk and yard around the nursery-school entrance. Mrs. Landrum, the wife of one of the principals, lugs rocks with us. The Landrums, with their little girl, live in a barrack like the rest of us. They don't have to, but they do. They're swell.

And we're getting the big boys to build cages in front of our nursery school and bring prairie creatures to put in them: a bull-snake, a prairie-dog, a gopher. With zoo and slides and swings, the children think this is a kind of overgrown picnic, and the mothers can hardly catch them long enough to wash them and change their clothes.

Tame animals are coming into camp, too. A taxi-driver brought a family of kittens, and everyone made a dash after them, both for pets and mousers. Field-mice are invading the barracks: pretty little white-stomached things, but you know how folks are about mice. It would seem more like home with Skippy, and I can't forget him. It must have seemed like a regular Pearl Harbor trick.

Kim says he'll get me some minnows tomorrow ——

Kim swung the scrub-bucket as he set out next morning. The day passed. The supper gong rang. No Kim appeared.

'Strange,' said Mrs. Ohara, 'when they're so strict about the eight-hour day here.'

'Probably the fish,' Sue answered comfortably. 'Maybe he got Mr. Martin and the fellows to help him, when half-past four came. He might catch enough to put in the big candy jar the Co-op let me have for the kindergarten, and some left over for the pool in our flower-box.'

Sue and her mother finally went to supper without Kim. 'It is such good beef today,' Mother said regretfully.

The food had improved. On a daily allowance of forty-five cents a person, most of the meat was third grade, of course, and Amache orders were usually filled after all others, so that when the stewards ordered pork, it often turned out to be wieners.

Mrs. Ohara and Sue lingered over their plates till only a few people were left at the tables, here and there an old man and an old woman, eating slowly, without much to say to each other. At length the mother and sister gave up and went home, where Sue wrote to Father and Mrs. Ohara worked on shades for the bed-lights.

The November dusk had thickened to dark when the door burst open and Kim limped in, one arm over Shig's shoulder, one leg stiff with bandages.

Sue sat with her mouth open and her pen hanging above the page. Mother sprang to Kim's side, handwork dropping to the floor where she crushed it beneath unheeding feet.

'Kimio!' she cried, seizing his arm and helping him toward the couch. 'Son, are you — are you all right?'

'Sure,' said Kim, letting himself down gingerly, leg stiffly extended. 'Fine, barring blood-poison, and that might be an easy out.'

'Shut up, bo,' Shig advised. 'There won't be any trouble, Mrs. Ohara. The bullet ——'

Sue shrieked, 'Bullet? Kim, you didn't try to escape?'

'What would be the good?' Kim growled, his face twisting with pain.

'Well, then what —? Oh, Kim, what happened?'

The boys told. Mrs. Ohara sat at Kim's side, her hands tightly clasped in her lap. Sue knelt to examine the bandage, sat back on her heels to listen, whispered, 'Why, the wretched dim-wit!' or, 'Good grief!'

The crew had been working at a far edge of the project, where it bordered the railway. It was after four, and Phil Martin said, 'Make it snappy, boys, so we can finish

here,' and raced away with his chain till he was lost to
sight in a hollow. Just then an old car drove up, climbed
the railway embankment at a crossing, and stopped for
the driver to peer out at the surveyors.

'He steps on the gas,' stuttered Kim, 'and roars down
the road and stops abreast of us. We didn't quit, figuring
he was somebody who wanted a look at a bunch of sneak-
ing Japs. But Mike makes a funny noise and we look
around, and, good gosh, the man's climbing out of that
car with a gun.'

'Gun pointing straight at us,' Shig broke in. 'Gollies,
did we freeze! He'd braced himself and taken aim ——'

'And Shig hollers, "Hey, what's the gun for?"'

'And the man yells, "What you reckon it's for, con-
found your slippery yellow hides?" — He's shaking with
excitement. — "And it won't do you a lick of good to
talk," he says.'

'And then, if Akira didn't let loose a flood of Japanese,'
Kim put in, grimacing at the memory. 'Said afterward
he never noticed he wasn't talking English. And did it
make the guy mad! He settled the gun on his shoulder
and ——'

'But why didn't you tell him?' Sue stuttered.

'Gosh, we did. I said, "Hold on, sir, we're from the
relocation camp. Our foreman's over there and he'll tell
you we're O.K." The man did take a look where I was
pointing, but you couldn't see hide or hair of Phil.'

Shig was laughing almost hysterically. 'Kim yells,
"Hey, I've got a brother serving overseas in the American
army. We're as good Americans as you are!" But that
only made the old fellow madder. I says, real low, "Let's
scatter!" and I screeched at the man, "Look, there's our
boss!" and waved toward where Phil had to be. Well, he
gives another look and we scatter, but there's no cover

and he gets Kim in the leg. He's reloaded and taken fresh aim when Phil comes panting up and knocks up his gun so the bullet goes over our heads ——'

'Mike thought he was shot and tripped on a wire and spraddled out in a bed of cactus,' Kim said, laughing. 'He's still picking out prickers.'

'By that time old Kim had bled all over the place and was looking kind of washed up. But the fellow with the gun wouldn't be satisfied with anything less than taking us to the police station. So Mike and I went ahead, half-carrying Kim, and Akira followed us, and then the traveler came stumping along, his jaw out, and Phil sticking close, to see he didn't try another shot.' Shig sighed reminiscently. 'And then, after the police surgeon dressed the young hero's honorable wound, Phil and an officer took us over to the hotel and hang the dirty looks of anyone who wanted to look dirty.'

'And we had steak,' Kim admitted.

'Oh, boy!' Shig said gloatingly.

'But the man with the gun,' Sue clamored.

Shig assumed an air of boredom. 'Oh, our impetuous friend? He stayed behind to cool off. In a nice cell.'

'Poor guy,' commented a voice behind Sue. She turned to look up into Jiro's eyes.

'My grief, Jiro!' she reproached him.

'Gosh, Kim, I'm sorry. But look at his side of it. Railroad track. Dam around the corner, maybe. We sinister little demons squinting down a tube. Dirty work! Sabotage! Blame him much for believing it?'

She could feel Kim's body relax at the easy, normal voice. She relaxed a little herself. But not enough. That night she lay stiff on her bed, thinking how easily the shot could have gone higher. Thinking what a threatening world it was for Oharas and Itos, outside the barbed wire. Thinking of the dark millions who had so often, throughout the years, been subject to such dangers in this land of the free. Thinking of the Jews, and of the pogroms that had killed so many of them in other countries ——

Behind Kim's partition the cot creaked as he turned and turned again, and once he gave the hoarse shout of a nightmare.

Had her ardent brother received wounds that would never heal? Would he ever be the same American again?

14

ZOOT SUITS

Kim's leg healed well, but Kim did not go back to work. Sometimes the family knew where he was, sometimes they did not. Sometimes he slept late behind his curtain, sometimes he was up and away at dawn. Sometimes he ate, sometimes he didn't. 'He's nothing but skin and bones,' Sue thought, her throat aching.

She herself was glad to have extra work to do, getting ready for the first block party. She and Choyo planned it, with Tomi helping, and sometimes Shig.

'Not that Tomi's much help,' Sue complained to Choyo. 'I don't know what's come over her. She was always quiet and Japanesy, but when we were in high school she did show a spark of life. Now she's a mouse. And getting still more Japanized.' The camp was afraid of being 'Japanized,' another new word in its vocabulary.

Choyo wrinkled her broad brow and blinked at Sue. 'Camp life does something to girls our age. There's no romance. There's nothing to expect.'

'Oh, fudge,' Sue protested.

'Well, you're sort of independent,' Choyo answered.
'And you've got your boy friend. Maybe it doesn't make
the same difference to you. But dating — and hoping to
meet someone wonderful — it's a big part of life in your
teens. And here courtship's like in an open cage. How
can you work up a tenderness? And there's nobody new
to meet.'

Startled, Sue thought, 'Why, it makes a lot of difference
to me, too. There isn't so much glamour about Jiro any
more, and maybe that's why. Just the thought of his
coming in our door used to make me dizzy, and when he
was playing football he stood out from the rest like an
electric light. Now I'd feel lost without him, but at
eighteen that's not enough. At home — oh, at home! —
each morning started an adventure. You never knew
what lovely, exciting thing might happen before night.
Here there's nothing waiting round the corner.'

Tomi continued to sit silent while the other girls
planned, and silently to cut papers and copy questions
for the games. And when the evening of the party came,
she silently pinned name-labels on the guests to hurry the
getting acquainted.

'Do you think we've got enough different things to do
to satisfy the different kinds of people?' Anxiously Sue
appealed to her companions as the party began. 'Your
phonograph ought to be almost enough by itself, Choyo.
Most of them like to dance, and there are lots of the latest
records as well as older ones. And the progressive games
— and the feeding-each-other races — and the refreshments ——'

The plans which had seemed so adequate were shrinking
to nothing, and it was too late to do anything about it.

'They're coming faster now. And look at that bunch
of fellows!' Choyo exclaimed. 'Their clothes!'

A dozen boys were slouching into the hall, four or five of them outlandishly arrayed. The revers of their bright blue or green or cinnamon-brown suits were fantastically wide. Coats were nipped in at the waist and hung to the knees. Trousers were so narrow at the ankle that Sue wondered how feet could squeeze through them.

'Zoot suits,' said Shig. 'Gosh, these are some tough guys who were just shifted in from other camps. There's that Marami kid. Jiro says the Maramis lived next door to them at Santa Anita, and their dad was interned.'

Zoot suit: glad plaid and reet pleat; yes, Sue knew name and song; but the suits themselves had not reached Cordova before evacuation; nor had Sue seen any at Santa Anita. She wished, uneasily, that Jiro were here; his hospital shift did not end till ten. These boys had darting eyes and a swagger. She was glad when other young people trooped in, laughing and chattering.

This group buzzed over writing their names and reading aloud those that were new to them, and responded when the phonograph invited them to a one-step. Meantime the zoot-suiters and their companions lounged in a corner and grinned.

'Know how they wrote their names?' Choyo snapped. 'Herbie the Hunk. Dannie the Dip. Like that.'

'Most unco-operative,' Sue said loftily.

'Sister, that ain't the half of it,' Shig assured her.

The broadest lapels shouldered their way through the room. 'How's about rug-cutting?' their wearer demanded.

He shut off the machine, tossed aside the record, thumbed through the stack and flipped on another disk. The zoot-suiters grabbed girls more or less willing, or paired with each other, whirling, leaping, swinging, bowing, hurling their partners from them, snapping them back, as in a mad game of Crack-the-Whip.

'My soul,' Sue protested to Shig. 'They swing it like a gang of toughs.'

'They are toughs,' Shig answered.

'Well, they needn't think ——' With Shig at her elbow, Sue marched over to the phonograph and shut it off with a click. 'Now if you'll all find seats at the tables,' she announced, spatting her hands together and shouting above the din, 'you'll find progressive games ——'

For a few minutes the games limped along, and then the phonograph began to blare more swing music, and Sue whirled to see Blue Lapels swaggering away from the instrument.

'Lay low,' Shig advised. 'We can't handle them. Some of our young country kids think the hoodlums are smart. They'd side with them. Look, Sue, there's your Taro ——'

The bleached boy was dancing hectically with a zoot-suiter. 'And there's Ike, the fellow Kim fought on the train,' said Sue. Then she gasped. '*And Kim.*'

Kim was dancing, too, flushed and with glittering eyes and not very expertly.

'Our evening is a dud,' Sue said heavily.

'Well, we'll know better next time,' said Choyo, keeping her eyes away from Kim. 'Why not serve our eats and call it a day?'

But when, a half-hour later, Sue, Choyo, Shig, and a tremulous Tomi passed refreshments, their worst moments began. Half-eaten sandwiches, plates, and cups flew round the room, and a splash of cocoa hit Sue in the face.

At that, Kim's lean tall body straightened and he grasped Blue Lapels by the shoulder. 'Hey!' he said, his voice cracking with protest. 'You're going too far!'

Blue Lapels jerked loose and tossed a fragment of sandwich.

Kim seized him again and whirled him toward the door. 'Get going, brother!' he gasped.

At once he was the center of a small mob, with girls milling round the edges, wringing their hands and shrieking. Sue squealed with relief when Jiro shouldered his way through the gang, flinging it right and left with his solid bulk.

Her relief was short-lived. The blue zoot-suiter hurled himself at Jiro like a wildcat. 'Here's the boy, fellows!' he snarled. 'One of them blasted Itos that turned in m'old man to the F.B.I.'

Sue pushed Tomi behind her and backed toward a corner. This was bad. Those hoodlums would have knives and brass knuckles — and where on earth were Shig and Choyo? Sue could not see them in the crowd flattened against the walls, nor amid the uncertain fringes.

Then, while everything whirled faster and faster, thudding and roaring, a heavy tread pushed through the tumult, and Mr. John strode in, Choyo and Shig close behind him. Mr. John's voice fell slow and calm on the uproar: 'Oh, come — come — come! Be human, sirs and madams.'

Pipe hanging lazily from the corner of his mouth, blue eyes sleepy, he elbowed his way into the thick of the scrimmage with negligent strong thrusts.

Sue giggled hysterically. Peachy-pink face, golden hair, heavy-lidded blue eyes now dangerous in their calm — and the zoot-suiters pulling themselves together, muttering, brushing dusty splendor and caressing bruised knuckles.

'Bid your little pals good night, gang,' Mr. John went on, arms akimbo, as he looked them wearily up and down. 'Toddle along to bed or papa might have to spank. Got

any of that cocoa for me, madams?' he finished, not turning to watch the zoot suits swagger limply away.

When the 'rec hall' had been put into a semblance of
order, Sue and Kim walked home with Jiro and Tomi.
Tomi's jaw sagging, Jiro's grim, Kim's lips tight and one
of his eyes beginning to discolor. Mr. Ito's head popped
above a partition when they entered, and he came out,
pulling a kimono about him, stuttering questions.

'Amache's got a gang,' Jiro said gruffly. 'Crashed the
party and broke it up. But the thing is, Father, those
Maramis say you turned in their old man.'

Jiro spoke in English. His father replied in Japanese
so rapid that Sue lost most of it, but his denial was unmistakable. No, he said sharply. He had never informed
on anyone. He wasn't the kind to cover his adherence to
Japan, his own country, by turning in someone else.

'Father! Your own country?' Jiro protested. '*My*
own country is America. I'd turn in anyone who was
traitor to her.'

Sue's heart tightened with sympathy. It was bad
enough — oh, bad enough indeed! — not to be sure of
your father's loyalty. But to be sure of his disloyalty —!

Mr. Ito waved helpless hands. Well, would America
let him be a citizen? he shouted. He could have been a
good citizen if America had not despised his yellow skin.

Jiro turned to the silent young Oharas. 'But my
father would not harm America. Not ever. And the
Japan he left was not this beastly, war-mad Japan ——'

'The Japan he left ——' Yes, Father had told them
about the changing Japan, for Cordova had no Japanese
language school, and he wanted his children to know their
own background. For centuries, he had said, the Japanese
were submissive: machines, wholly under the power of the
military. Then came the awakening to the outside world,

and for a few short years the trampled hordes began to
stand erect; began to think of democracy. Democracy!
the word flew like wildfire through the little paper houses.
During a few short years, before the military stamped the
hordes down again. And Mr. Ito, like most of the issei,
had come from the Japan of those few short years.

Mr. Ito passed a shaking hand across his mouth. 'No,'
he agreed, in English now, 'I would not ever harm this
country. Me — what have I left? Nothing. All is gone.
And I near seventy, too old for new starting.' He looked
long at the brick floor beneath his slippered feet. 'But
my chil'ren, they are Americans. America has throw
them off, but maybe she take them back again. Anyway,
we issei fathers, we not want to spoil those future for our
chil'ren. We not — how you say it? — gum the works for
nisei.'

Sue told her mother the story of the evening, and then
lay long awake, turning it over in her mind. Kim went
silently to his cot and Sue heard no sound from him. Except that just as she was sinking into sleep she roused for
an instant, thinking that she heard the door open and shut.

15

MOSTLY JIRO

The next day was Saturday. Mrs. Ohara had
gone to the laundry-house, and Kim, sleeping
too late to go to breakfast, had just dressed
and was hunched moodily reading on his cot,
his swollen eye green and blue. Sue was tidy-
ing up the apartment when someone knocked.
Opening the door, she looked up into the hard-hewn ruddy
face of Amache's chief of police.

'Miss Ohara?'

'Yes,' she stammered, because her head was whirling with fear. 'Is it about the block party, officer? Do you think we oughtn't to try it again? Are we too different?'

He shook his head, looking past her into the room. 'Parties are all right. We'll give them police protection after this. It's your brother I want to see.'

That was what Sue had feared. Silently she stood aside and motioned the officer to come in, and Kim gathered himself up from the cot. His face wore the veiled, unresponsive look that she had never seen there in the old days.

'What do you know about the fellows that kicked up the row last night?' the chief asked curtly.

'Practically nothing.'

'I understand you came with them.'

'I went with Taro,' Kim said thinly, grating the cot backward on the bricks. 'You might say I went with them. But I didn't go home with them.'

'So I heard,' the officer said with the shadow of a grin. 'Nice shiner the blue zoot suit gave you.' His tone sharpened. 'Did you make up with him afterward?'

Kim shook his head.

The chief turned to Sue. 'Your brother came home with you, Miss Ohara?'

Sue moistened her lips. 'Why, yes, he did. — Why — yes. And he went right to bed.' It seemed to Sue that the officer was watching her throat as she swallowed.

He stood stoutly on spread legs and his probing gray eyes turned to Kim. 'You're sure you haven't anything to tell me?'

Kim shook his head. 'No, sir. What would I have to tell?'

'You ought to know,' the chief snapped. 'We don't

want to get tough with you fellows. But up to now we've had a clean camp, and we mean to keep it that way. So far the property destroyed or taken has amounted to very little. It's looked like the work of a few sore kids. But last night —— '

Sue drew a quick breath. 'Last night?'

'The piano in Sperry Hall was smashed up,' he said.

'You think it might be those zoot-suit boys?' Sue asked tremulously.

He did not reply. 'Why did you quit your job?' he asked Kim. 'There's plenty of work that needs doing, here in camp, and any fellow's better off when he's busy. Things are a lot likelier to run smooth if everybody's working.'

'I didn't like being shot at,' Kim said sullenly. 'My wages wouldn't pay for a funeral.'

'Well, mind your step, young man,' the chief advised, and strode through the door and away.

When Sue turned from closing the door, Kim was already sprawled on the couch again and buried in his book. He would not meet her eyes. She opened her mouth to speak, and closed it again. She could not even ask, 'Kim, did you get up and go out again last night?' How could she imply a suspicion of Kim — *Kim?* But the question settled down upon her like black fog.

From that day on she plunged deeper into the camp activities. School first. All the teachers, from Mr. Sperry, the superintendent, down to Sue and the other assistants, were redoubling their efforts to make the flimsy barracks pleasant. They would continue to house all the grades up to high school.

A wave of Caucasian anger had swept away the elementary and junior high buildings which had been planned. The lowest bid for the three structures, temporary though they were, had been a third of a million dollars, and protests against the extravagance were so vehement as to stop construction of all but the high school. The materials for the other two lay where they were, and the contractors rolled up their sleeves to sue for the amount of the contract.

'Who's any better off?' Sue said stormily. 'The Government pays — for nothing. And the youngsters get nothing. And how was it our fault? They act as if we were the ones to make money on those contracts. And as if we asked to come here.'

'Someone's always saying, "Why did you have to come to America in the first place?"' Choyo put in.

'And why did they have to come in the first place? The Indians never asked them to.'

'What makes me saddest,' said Mrs. Fennell, deftly lettering word-charts, 'and maddest, is that our best chance to bring up a set of loyal Americans is through good, efficient schools. Seems as if we muff our chance when we handicap the schools.'

But her clear eyes, boyish under her gray hair, and her smiling mouth and tilted nose rebounded to optimism. She sighed and laughed. 'I guess if the little red schoolhouse could build up a democracy, the little barracks schoolhouse can follow suit. If only we never have a fire!'

As winter came on, the children simmered on the side next the old army stove and shivered on the side next the drafty windows, just as children had done in pioneer days. They had a great many colds, and crowded the camp hospital with light cases of pneumonia. But there were no schoolhouse fires. The fire department held themselves ready and boasted of their record of no important blazes in the tinderbox camp.

School took Sue's first attention, and the Y.W.C.A.

Hospitality House, which lived up to its name, even inside four blank barrack walls. Finally, Sue threw herself into the task of furnishing the home apartment.

Jiro, finishing the frames for the Oharas' bamboo curtains, one day, watched her absorption anxiously. 'Sumiko,' he asked, pausing midstroke with a wad of steel wool, 'how come you changed your mind? You're licking into this now as if you meant to stay. Even your little eyebrows are tied in a hard knot ——'

Mrs. Ohara, writing a letter, cleared her throat.

Sue said, 'Well, if Father is let out ——' There it was again, the bitter doubt: for if Father had not been pro-Japan at all, then why were they holding him so long? And if he had been —? 'If Father is let out, there's no telling how long he and Mother would be here. Because what would Father get relocated *to?*' she asked heavily. 'You have to have school or a job, to get out.'

'Plenty of fine jobs offered, so the newspapers say.'

'Listen.' Sue picked up the mimeographed Amache paper, the *Pioneer*. '"Job opportunities: Four warehouse workers, Cleveland. Kitchen workers, Chicago. Three housemen, Chicago. Expert cook and housekeeper, Chicago." What's there for Dad? All he knows is plants, and he isn't too young and strong. Why, even for me I don't see anything.'

'I wish Tomi would get a housework job and go to college,' Jiro said, 'or business school.'

Sue flushed. 'Housework — Mother says I don't even make beds well. I've always been busy with other things.'

'And Kim?' Jiro asked, running his hand over the pine frame and tilting his head to eye the mellow surface.

Sue stitched fast. 'Kim — he's drawn into his shell like a crab.'

'Well, it would be a jolt to be shot.'

'Coming on top of other things,' she assented. 'It's —
turned Kim upside down. He doesn't think there's any
use trying. And he won't stick his nose outside Amache.'

Jiro flowed clear lacquer on the satiny wood and murmured: 'Girl, doesn't that go double? Are you letting it
get your pluck, too? You settling down here?'

'Well, my grief, what about you?' Half-amused and
half-stung, Sue dropped the curtains she was hemming
and stared at him. 'Haven't you been working like a
demon to get your place fixed up? Ours, too?'

'It's my folks.' Jiro frowned as he edged the brush
deftly down a crack. 'They're so set. And it's not wasted
time. I get a lot out of my hospital work. But, Sue ——'
With mild exasperation he glanced at the neat top of Mrs.
Ohara's head, bent above her swift pen. 'Sue,' he said,
'how about making a wooden awning for that window?'

Sue's mouth flew open in surprise, but Jiro smiled
meaningly toward the door.

'Why, yes,' said Sue, getting to her feet as Mrs. Ohara's
pen paused. 'This sunny west window, Jiro?'

Jiro laid down his brush and followed her outside.
'Like this,' he said, slanting his long, strong hand down at
an angle from the window top, while his eyes smiled into
Sue's. 'Listen, Sumiko, if you're really planning to stay
here, won't you — think again about what I said in Santa
Anita that last night?'

Sue wasn't looking at him. She was responding de-
murely to the bow of an old man who was passing.

'Sue, couldn't our lives be happier if we —?'

'How is your brother now, Sumiko?' called a woman
who lived on the other side of the camp.

'Thank you, Mrs. Watobe, Kim's wound is entirely
healed. And how are you? I think the awning's a swell
idea, Jiro,' she went on mischievously, turning back to

Jiro and the window. 'But you can see Mother's doubtful about it.'

'Sue, I could wring your little neck.'

'Like the tough lovers in the movies?'

Jiro repeated his act of outlining an awning in the air, for the benefit of Mrs. Ohara, who had sat back from her letter-writing to watch. 'Answer me, Sue!' he said, his eyebrows fierce.

Sue sobered. 'Jiro, I don't think I feel the way I ought to. You're dear, but you're dear like a brother.'

'I don't feel like any brother,' Jiro muttered, measuring off the window, crossly, as another neighbor approached, feet lisping on the gravel in issei fashion, and paused to see what they were doing. Presently she went on, her hands sliding down to her knees as she bent in the ceremonious issei bow to Mrs. Ohara at the window.

'How can I court you American style here?' Jiro gestured widely, as if the proposed awning were to take in all Amache, and Mrs. Ohara looked puzzled and suspicious. 'Especially when your mother won't give me a chance. I'd like to tell you that your eyebrows are little wings and your mouth a pomegranate bud and ——'

'Don't be quaint,' Sue ordered, though she felt a secret pleasure. 'That sounds Japanese, and I'm not Japanese.' To her dismay, her face twisted. 'I'm not Japanese, and it seems I'm not American. It's awful, not being anything.'

Jiro studied her, his arm suspended in air. 'It isn't our social class that's the trouble, Sue? I'm learning to use the right fork — have you noticed? It isn't that?'

Sue shook her head. 'How can you live with millionaires and — and hucksters, without getting to know that folks are folks? But it's true that our fathers don't — don't approve of each other.'

'My father's softened up a lot since you and Kim went

to bat for us the night of the party,' Jiro said, his eyes
narrowing with laughter and his strong white teeth flashing.

'Jiro, we've got to go in,' Sue said hastily. 'Mother's
got the fidgets, and look at those junior highs.'

Jiro scowled and then grinned at four ribbon-tied braids
jerking out of sight around a corner.

'We've decided to wait till after Christmas to build the
awning,' Sue said as they re-entered the room.

'Oh? I thought you must have finished building it,'
Mrs. Ohara commented dryly.

Mrs. Ohara had not softened toward Jiro, Sue thought
unhappily. She was always coolly courteous to him, and
at least she did not forbid him the house. But the more he
did for them, the more firmly Mrs. Ohara set herself against
him, as if she were afraid of liking him against her will.

If it were not for the parental dislike, Sue thought, it
might be better to marry Jiro and make what she could of
life inside the barbed wire. If it were not for the parental
dislike. Was she, the independent Sue Ohara, growing
Japanized, too?

16

FATHER

Holiday trimmings! Schoolrooms and mess
halls vied with each other to make a cheerful
display. Wreaths were fashioned from dried
sagebrush dipped in green paint and studded
with poinsettias which were milkweed pods
flattened out and painted scarlet. Colored
yucca pods and shavings and curls of wood formed quaint
festoons. In Sperry Hall shone a decorated Christmas

tree, sent by a Denver church. And boxes kept coming: boxes of clothing, old and new, boxes of Sunday School supplies, boxes of gifts, gay with tissue and ribbon and seals.

The Amache Oharas had sent a Christmas box to Tad's A.P.O. address, a box that held even his joke pretzels, and packages to Father and Amy. One had come from Amy, but none from the others.

In the early dusk two days before Christmas, the family had settled themselves for letter-writing, reading, and the last handwork on Christmas gifts, when a soft knock sounded at their door. Kim went and threw it open, his book closed on one finger. Then he stood still.

Sue looked up from her letter, saying, 'Isn't there anyone there?' and shrieked, 'Dad!' and rushed to draw him inside. Mother rose with an audible gasp, color staining the ivory of her face. Smiling, Father came in.

After the first shaken greetings, they urged him down on the divan and crowded round him, taking off his overcoat, carrying away his hat.

'You look — pretty well,' Mother said. 'But the gray hair is new.'

'Nothing was really bad except ——' Father tossed an expressive hand which seemed to take in his family, his business, the lost work of years.

'Father, why did they keep you so long?' Sue asked. She hadn't meant to ask, and now she felt dizzy, as if she had run out upon a shaky trestle.

Father looked at her gravely. 'They held me until they had made sure, beyond a doubt, that my record was as — as American as my heart and conscience,' he said.

Sue sat gulping and trembling. She had crossed the trestle and was on solid ground again after all these unsure months.

Kim, though, sat scowling and roughing his hair with a nervous hand. 'And nothing against you — nothing?' he burst out. 'Dad, how could they be so unjust?'

'It is different in time of war,' Mr. Ohara said slowly. 'It was necessary to make thorough investigation of those who had continued to show interest in Japan.' He frowned anxiously at Kim. 'You are thin,' he said. 'You are more changed than the rest.' No one answered, and he asked, 'When have you heard from Tad?'

'Too long,' said Mother. 'But tomorrow, I think.'

For the first time she looked down, uncomfortably, at her clothing. Mother in slacks was quaintly funny: her Japanese lady's head surmounted a slender boy's body. Father's glance followed hers.

'The children,' she murmured. 'It is much easier to climb over our eating benches ——'

'It is all right,' Father said, smiling. 'And this room is beautiful.'

It was beautiful. The bamboo shades, hung from Jiro's pine frames, formed a small living room and showed only misty shapes of beds and wardrobes beyond. Jiro had made the low divan and the coffee-table before it. With glowing amber pine, box-garden with pool and plants, scarlet bridge chairs from 'Monkey-Ward,' the room had color and style.

Next day the Oharas' cup of joy was full, for a letter came from Tad. One came also from Mr. Clemons. He thought it might increase their Christmas happiness, he said, to know that the church had secured one scholarship for them.

The young Oharas sat silent when Mr. Clemons's letter was read. Father looked at them quickly. 'Where's your Yankee enthusiasm?' he asked. 'I thought a scholarship — college ——'

'Dad,' Kim replied harshly, 'did it ever occur to you that your starry-eyed infants might grow up? Find out their dolls were stuffed with sawdust, and all that junk?'

Mr. Ohara sighed and rubbed the top of his head thoughtfully. The grizzled hair was even thinner than it had been a year ago. 'Let's be happy on Christmas Eve,' he said, wistfully.

'Last Christmas Eve ——' Kim began.

'Last Christmas Eve?' Sue rallied him. 'The only thing that was better about it was being at home. You have to go back another year to get to our Age of Innocence, my dear little brother. The year before Pearl Harbor. Before Tojo killed Santa Claus. But tonight's going to be swell, Dad. I'm going caroling with a bunch of church kids. Last year this camp site didn't hear anything but coyotes, and this year it will be treated to antique Christmas carols in the best modern style.'

Up and down the Amache streets went the carolers under the piercing-bright stars, and barrack doors were thrown open to let in the strains of 'Silent Night,' of 'We, Three Kings,' of 'The First Noël.'

And next morning the Oharas ate their Christmas breakfast at the card-table. The Clemonses had boxed and sent their electric grill and waffle iron and percolator, and now that Amache could use electrical appliances without blowing out many fuses, Mother was able to brew coffee and make waffles with boxed waffle-mix. Never had a breakfast tasted more delicious. They ate and beamed and opened their few gifts and looked at their Christmas cards and letters. Cordova was well represented, and there were cards from Miss Saito, and the young fireman, and from Mrs. Filkins, already relocated with her slightly Japanese family.

In the evening Father and Mother and Sue strolled out under the high, glittering stars.

'Where is Kim?' Mr. Ohara asked, when Mother locked the door after them.

'He has his own key.' Mother gave a small sigh. 'It is not like being at home, where parents can keep track of their young folks' coming and going.'

'In good company, do you think?' Father asked.

'Not with Shig very much any more, nor with Jiro,' Sue said. 'Father, I hope you can do something about Kim. I'm so afraid ——'

'As your mother says, the home is broken, its influence at least.'

Half unconsciously, Sue had led the way toward the Ito barrack and now slowed her steps before it, seeing Tomi at the door. As Sue called a greeting, Jiro came and looked out over his sister's head, smiling.

'Couldn't we stop a few minutes?' Sue implored.

Father tightened his lips, and Mother's shoulders stiffened, but Mr. and Mrs. Ito came out to invite them in, and, coolly polite, they went down the steps from the street and into the apartment.

Seated in the room which had started life as a twin of the Oharas', Sue looked anxiously at her parents to see whether they were appreciating it. Jiro had built substantial screen frames, set on broad bases, and covered them with the Viofilm manufactured for the poultry house. The uneven translucence of that humble stuff lent a gracious luminous glow to the room, as from handmade glass. The curtains and bedspreads were of flounced gingham. Sue and Jiro together had argued Tomi out of slick rayon. Altogether the Ito room was as lovely as the Oharas'.

'Jiro's going to make a table, too,' Sue told her father. 'They did one in Home Ec, out of a lumbering old messhall table. They sort of unevened the edges and the cross-pieces, and then painted those scallopy edges a bright blue after they'd rubbed the wood down and stained it. Then they rubbed it down some more and waxed it and you'd never guess how it had started out. Jiro's is going to be even prettier.'

In issei style, Mr. and Mrs. Ito bowed again and again to Mr. and Mrs. Ohara, but most to Father. Sue was embarrassed at the deference, annoyed because the broad, opaque faces hid any dislike they might feel. Now Mrs. Ito boiled tea-water on an electric plate Jiro had managed to find for her, and Tomi and Mitsu passed wafers.

Mr. Ito took from the table a pair of socks still lying in their Christmas tissue, and held them toward Father, half-smiling. 'A present for me,' he said in Japanese. 'The first Christmas present of my life. From a church, too. I have not been friendly to Christian churches. Yet it is the Christians who have been kindest to us at a time like this ——'

Jiro cleared his throat and spoke, his voice young and strong across the older voices. 'I, too,' he said. 'I did not think this Christianity had anything to do with me. I had not seen it working much in the white people. But now it is different. And since last night I have been thinking. I have been thinking that when this preacher baptizes followers of Christ, as he says he will, I shall be one who follows.'

It was a long speech for laconic Jiro. When he had done, his mother shifted her eyes to the closed face of his father. Mr. Ito contemplated his son for a moment. 'I do not forbid,' he said at last.

'And it wouldn't do you a speck of good if you did!' Sue thought exultantly.

'My friend, your son and daughter call themselves

Christians,' Mr. Ito said to Father, 'and I do not dislike
what they are. They have stood by us in difficulties.
One day I hope the Itos may serve the Oharas. I hope
our families may be friends.'

Mr. Ohara's bow was as deep as Mr. Ito's, but his
words were politely noncommittal.

Going home with the Milky Way a white glory above
them, Sue thought her father's unresponsiveness the day's
only flaw.

'Oh, Father,' she begged, her fingers tightening on his
arm, 'don't you like the Itos better now? Don't you?'

Father was slow to answer.

'Don't you, Dad?' she persisted.

'I think this Jiro might be all right,' Father said slowly.
'But the stock from which a man springs, Daughter —
that is important, too.'

17

THE TELEGRAM

The telegram came in late January. Jiro, now
on night shift at the hospital, had walked home
from school with Sue. The two quickened
their steps when they saw a man waiting at the
Ohara door.

'It's the officer from the Internal Security
Office,' Jiro said.

Sue's mouth went dry. 'It wouldn't be something
about — Kim. No, he has an — an envelope.'

She didn't know what she said when the man handed
her the yellow envelope. Jiro's strong hand closed on her
arm, steadying her.

'Now wait,' he told her. 'It could be a lot of things. Your business. Your house.'

'It's Tad,' she said dully.

'Well, supposing it is. It could be a little wound. In this war wounds don't mean much. Wait till you read it, Sumiko.'

The Ohara apartment was empty. Sue recalled that her mother had gone to the wash-house, and she went after her, head dizzy and stomach whirling. Jiro thought Mr. Ohara might be playing *goh* with some of the men. He would find him. He thought he could find Kim, too, he said with a hesitancy that Sue noticed even then.

Sue and her mother returned first, Mrs. Ohara's hands dripping unnoticed on her immaculate house dress. She moved the chairs about, averting her eyes from the yellow envelope on the table.

'Mother, please open it,' Sue quavered.

Mother shook her head.

Steps in the entry heralded Kim and Father. Kim's eyes leaped ahead to the telegram. Behind him, Jiro was saying, 'Well, good-bye, then.'

With automatic politeness Father said, 'Stay, please.'

Sue begged, 'Oh, Jiro, please.'

So Jiro went over and leaned against the wall.

Father slit the envelope, with difficulty because it shook and rattled so, and took out the enclosure. Mother stood beside him, and their eyes rushed along the message.

After a minute, Father bent his knees stiffly, feeling behind him with one hand for the chair. He flattened the paper on the table and sat staring at the blank wall with a strained smile on his lips and a look in his eyes as of one who tries to comprehend something beyond his grasp. Mother — Mother might have been gripped by an unbearable pain which she must keep behind the smooth

mask of her face. Or she might have been thinking of a
crochet pattern. She dropped her eyes and stood motionless.

'My little clock?' Sue wondered suddenly. 'Why do I
hear it ticking when I never could hear it before?' But it
was not her clock; it was the blood thudding in her ears.

Out of the silence Kim spoke thickly. 'I've got to
enlist,' he said, springing to his feet. 'I've got to take his
place. Now surely they'll make an exception ——'

His father's and mother's eyes came to him as if they
had forgotten that they had a son Kimio. Jiro, who had
been effacing himself there by the window, strode over and
threw an arm across Kim's shoulders as he plunged toward the door. 'I'll go along,' Jiro said.

The spell of silence broken, Sue looked at Mrs. Ohara's
blanched face and said, 'Mother, you need some tea ——'
getting up from the divan with the words. Through
minutes that stood still, she plugged in the electric grill,
boiled water, swished it around the teapot to warm it ——

Automatically, Mr. and Mrs. Ohara sipped their tea,
while Sue stood above them, staring at the typed capitals
pasted on the yellow paper:

THE SECRETARY OF WAR . . . HIS DEEP REGRET . . .
YOUR SON, PVT. TADASHI OHARA . . . KILLED IN
ACTION . . . DECEMBER 22 . . . SILVER STAR ——

When they were reading his last letter, then, it had already happened. His latest letter: no, his last letter.
Already gone — gone — gone. He never got this year's
pretzels, Sue thought irrelevantly, and was pierced with
pain because he had not. How they had feuded with each
other, she and Tad. About the last cooky on the plate.
About Sue's short skirts and her lipstick and whether her

wine-colored fingernails looked like claws. About Tad's girls, whether they were lovelies or only beautiful and dumb.

In that last letter he had said: 'I read that skirts are shorter than ever. For Pete's sake, Sue, everybody knows girls have knees. You don't have to prove it.' Sue had written back that he ought to see one of his best girls, the one who had been sent to Amache, and the dress she was wearing.

Sue sobbed. Tad wasn't the kind of boy that died. Died a hero. *Died.* Why, Tad was just maddening and dear. If Tad was gone, the Ohara family was breaking up.

Mrs. Ohara rose like a puppet and stacked the two cups with excessive attention. She sifted soap into the toy dishpan Sue had got her, poured in water from the tea-kettle, washed the dishes ——

Outside, feet dragged across the entry bricks. Kim and Jiro came in.

Sue said, 'They wouldn't take you.'

'We're still classified Enemy Aliens,' Jiro said — '4–C.'

'We?'

'I thought I might as well try it, too.' Looking into Sue's eyes, Jiro shook Kim's shoulder and went out.

That day came old friends and new, made in Santa Anita and here. They sat on divan and little chairs, without much to say. The girl with the checked skirt switching above slim knees — the girl Sue had mentioned in that last letter — did not come. Once when Sue called to her she slipped away between the barracks and Sue saw her walking fast, shoulders bent as if the warm midwinter sunshine were a blizzard.

People said haltingly: 'Sue, I wouldn't give up hope. They do make mistakes. I knew a boy whose folks got

word — like this — from the War Department, and at
that very time he was home on furlough ——'

Even Shig muttered, 'Could be another Tadashi Ohara,
Sue.'

But after the first attempts, people stopped trying to
comfort Kim.

18

KIM

Kim avoided his friends and his family. On heavy
feet he would clump into the apartment after
the rest of the Oharas were abed. He would
answer their greetings with monosyllables, and
presently they would hear the shriek of his cot
as he got in, and its groan as he turned over
and over. It was worse when they heard nothing: the
silence of a tense body and controlled breathing.

And then came a morning when Mrs. Ohara, looking
behind Kim's screen, found his muslin and calico spread
drawn smooth and round over his pillow. She turned
dumbly to the others, motioning toward the unused bed.
Sue dropped her comb and ran out into the chill blackness
of morning, toward the Ito quarters. No, the Itos had
not seen him. No, Jiro was not here. They thought he
had gone straight to breakfast from the hospital.

It was not until Sue was turning into the school block
that morning that she saw her brother, haggard and
bowed, slouching homeward.

She found school in a flurry of excitement, small groups
forming, murmuring, breaking up, teachers pausing to

exchange words. Mrs. Fennell soon explained the commotion.

'The Junior Hi Co-op was broken into last night,' she said. 'Isn't it a shame, when it was doing so well?'

Sue stared silently at Mrs. Fennell.

'Yes, they took the money that was in the till, and a lot of merchandise. All the Amache Indian T-shirts, and two American flags. Of all things to steal! How do you suppose they expected to dispose of them?'

Sue moistened her lips, arranged her voice. 'Maybe it was the remnants of that zoot-suit gang,' she suggested.

'Or the Yellow-Shirts. Could be. It's a pity, when Amache's had such a good record — only one or two of the other camps as good. You'd think Mr. Sperry'd lost his last friend. He's carried everything with such a high heart, I don't know what we'd do if he were to get down himself.'

'Don't you think there's a kind of strain —?' Sue asked, wondering at herself for being able to think and speak at all. 'It does seem as if there's a tension that wasn't here at first.'

Mrs. Fennell nodded soberly. 'Too much is bottled up — worries — resentments — sorrows.   And there isn't anything constructive for most of the people to do. Just marking time. You put it another way, and these young folks are uprooted trees. If you get them back into good ground quick enough, they may go on making normal growth. But we aren't getting them back quick. Yes, you see it in their not wanting to work at jobs they don't like. It's as if they were saying — "Well, you brought me here, I guess you can look out for me whether I work or not." It's logical enough, but it isn't healthy.' She stopped, her cheerful mouth drawn self-consciously straight. Kim wasn't working ——

Kim wasn't working. Kim was hanging around the canteen with Taro and his friends. Kim was sitting on his cot reading what he could find on the scantily filled shelves of the Amache library; reading, and flinging the magazine or book across the room in a burst of wrath. Kim was a creature of heights and depths, and now the depths had him.

And Kim hadn't come home last night.

Sue made herself follow Mrs. Fennell into the Co-op. The end of a school barrack was partitioned off and fitted with a tidy counter and shelves where school supplies, stationery, *Reader's Digest* and *Scholastic* were displayed, and bakery goods three times a week. The store was doing a good business, and it was a constructive activity, besides, fitting practically into social science studies and math.

Boys and girls were thronging it now, selecting doughnuts, frosted cupcakes, ham sandwiches — those who had any money. They were always hungry, and the home cooky jar, bread box, and refrigerator were missing in Amache.

Today their interest was divided between their purchases, the lawlessness of the night before, and the question whether they would lose their dividends on their membership investments, since so much money and stock had been taken. The young clerks importantly pointed out shattered window and emptied shelf, and the room rocked with indignation.

Sue said, 'Mrs. Fennell, I wonder if you could excuse me this morning.'

'Why, Sue, how pale you are! Go on home and rest awhile, child. We'll manage without you.'

The uproar died behind Sue as she started away. These youngsters, at least, she thought with half her mind, did

not seem warped by evacuation, or at any rate not in-
hibited. When they had been sandwiched in between
Caucasian children who far outnumbered them, they had
been remarkably quiet. Now, if less exemplary, they were
more natural.

Sue slowed her steps to speak to Mary Kaneko, crouch-
ing in front of a cage where a snake coiled and uncoiled.
'Mustn't seem hurried and worried,' Sue thought, feeling
as if unseen eyes were upon her.

Beside Mary her pet dog sat trembling, the hair on end
along its spine as it watched. 'Listen at it snore!' Mary
said, intent on the long hiss and gentle indrawing of
breath, but moving to make room for Sue. 'Look at him!
he's rounding up again' — as the long body flowed into
its spiral heap. 'But nevah caih, Sue,' she added in the
current Amache slang, 'he can't get out.'

Sue patted Mary and hurried on. Mary wasn't worried any more about whether she was a person. Kiku had
almost forgotten about going back to America. The
children under fourteen or fifteen were settling down to
being camp Japanese. And what would that mean to
their future? While on the other hand there were the
Kims and the Taros ——

When she reached home, she found her father reading
the *Pioneer* and her mother darning a pair of Kim's socks,
placing exquisite stitches over and under in a perfection
of weaving.

Sue could hardly wait to tell them what she feared.
'Father! Mother!' she began brokenly.

Before she could say more, a tap at the door interrupted
her. Jiro stood there, looking at the floor. Sue's heart
bumped lower.

'Sir,' Jiro said respectfully '— ma'am — I hope you
won't think I'm butting in, but I've got to say this.

About Kim. I think the world of Kim. And I'm afraid
he ——'

Sue said tensely: 'You think he was in that gang last
night, Jiro Ito? And you call yourself his friend? — Oh,
Jiro,' she rushed on illogically, 'you know it would be only
because he was crazy with grief, crazy because his own
country hasn't any use for him. So he thinks, well, then,
what difference does it make —?'

Jiro regarded her steadily, all the twinkle and quirk
erased from his bronzed face. Father and Mother said,
'What gang, Sumiko?' 'Daughter, what are you saying?'

Tumultuously she told of the night's robbery — the
Amache Indian T-shirts, the flags — and when the three
listeners stared in shocked silence, she pleaded, 'He isn't
himself. All his love and patriotism have been kept inside him. They've burned him out. Maybe nothing
would seem too outrageous, too — too opposite to his
real personality ——'

'You ought to know better!'

Sue's eyes jerked toward Jiro in amazement. It was
she, Sue, whom his words were lashing.

'The Taros, the zoot-suit boys, yes. But not Kim.
People keep their own patterns, even when they're
thrown off balance. A tree falls the way it's grown.'

Sue said, 'But you don't know how deep it's cut.'

'Don't I?' Jiro asked somberly. 'But it won't make
Kim forget the laws he's been brought up in. It won't
do anything to Kim but break his heart and spoil his life.'

Father's paper rustled in his twitching hands. 'I think
you are right,' he said. 'But what can we do?'

'Believe in him, in the first place,' Jiro answered, his
eyes on Sue.

Sue's small nod was decisive.

'Till I went on duty last night,' Jiro continued, 'Kim

and I were up at the high-school site, chewing the rag —
excuse me, talking. And then I took him on to the hospital with me. Your house was dark, so I thought you'd
all be asleep. And Kim was — sort of desperate.'

'He was with you all night,' Sue whispered.

'Yes. Talking about whether he should join up with
the new Japanese-American Combat Unit.'

They broke in: 'But he tried —— ' 'I thought —— '

'Mr. John told him: President Roosevelt has said the
nisei should be allowed to volunteer.'

There was a sibilance of escaping breath in the room.

'And my son — he is very glad?'

Jiro shook his head. 'Not now. Because they would
not accept him before. Because it is a segregated unit,
all Japanese. Besides, he says, America has deprived us
of our civil liberties, so why should we offer our lives for
her? But I think it would cure Kim of his sickness.'

'And are you going to volunteer?' Sue asked.

Jiro seemed to sag. 'My mother —— ' he said. 'She
is very Japanese. She says I am no longer her son if I
volunteer. And I can serve otherwise. It is different
with Kim. He is sick. Really sick.'

Sue thought, 'That is it: many of us are growing sick;
abnormal; even when it does not show so plainly as in
Kim. Tomi, fading to a colorless shadow. Father, doing
nothing but sit; not even playing *goh* any more. I, afraid
to step outside this safe imprisonment. And Jiro — even
Jiro.'

She spoke almost violently: 'I won't stay here any longer.
I'll get my application for relocation today.'

Jiro asked, 'College? Your scholarship?'

'No,' Sue said abruptly; 'you take the scholarship.
You or Tomi.' She thought, 'You because you're worth
it, Tomi because it might be her one chance to be a real
person.'

'And what about you, daughter?' Mr. Ohara asked.

'I'll — do housework and pay my way through college.' Sue's voice was firmer than her feelings. 'There's nothing to be ashamed of in housework. It's snobbish to think there is. You could be a doctor that much sooner, Jiro, and we need doctors.'

Jiro straightened his sagging shoulders. 'I'm volunteering,' he said. 'If you're willing to go outside and do housework — I'm volunteering. Mr. John thinks I could get into a medical unit.' Jiro was smiling at Sue, but gravely. That was because of his mother, she thought, whom he loved.

In the small entry which had already known so many sad steps, so many weary steps, sounded the scrape and shift of boots. Kim stood in the door, listening. His family turned anxious faces toward him.

'My son!' — Mr. Ohara's voice shook — 'you could have come home and explained to us.'

'Oh, Kim!' Sue wailed. 'We were afraid ——'

'I should think you'd have got used to my tramping around by myself — oh, and loafing with Taro and such fellows. I've been a darn fool, but I've taken it out in talk. I suppose you were afraid I'd try the quick way out.'

Sue drew a sharp breath.

'Whenever I thought of that, I'd picture the headlines. They'd say, JAP COMMITS HARI-KIRI. That was too Japanese a gesture. And now I'm glad I didn't. Jiro, if you're volunteering, then I am, too.'

19

SHINING DAY

Sue's day had dawned in black misery. The flamboyant sunrise had seemed a mockery when she stepped out of the Junior Hi Co-op. Now her whole sky flamed as bright as that splendid east.

In the afternoon, when the workmen had laid by their tools, she and Tomi, Kim, and Jiro walked up to the site of the high school. The four stood on the height, Jiro quiet, Tomi uncomprehending, Kim haggard but with face at peace. Sue thought, 'I've changed places with Kim again. Wonderful to feel your spirits go up — up — up! But frightening, too. I'm glad it doesn't often happen to me.'

With a small, sobbing chuckle, she came up on her toes, chin high, arms out in an unconscious gesture that took in her brother, her friends, Amache and the world beyond. 'The sky!' she said breathlessly. 'The white road!'

Purple-shadowed under the high blue, as on the morning when Jiro came into Amache, the road led out to the river valley. There the lengthening sun-rays had fired the bare trees, making their netted branches a cloud of glory.

'Cottonwoods are as beautiful as eucalyptus and live oaks,' Sue said wonderingly. 'And now it's as if life were rising in them.'

'Amache will be better, too,' Jiro said, 'when our people set the little Chinese elms and box elders along the streets and make little Victory gardens at their doors.'

'Mr. Kaneko showed me his drawings for a miniature garden. There'll be a lot of those, too,' said Kim.

'We're really the newest pioneers,' Sue said in a hushed

145

voice. 'We, the evacuees, the moved-outers. We're American patriots, loving our country with our hearts broken. And those who must can be pioneers behind barbed wire, but those who can must go out and pioneer in the wide world.'

From somewhere near at hand a bird-call came fluting.

'Listen!' said Sue. 'Not a mockingbird, but——'

'It's a robin,' said Jiro. 'Robins and cottonwoods are part of America, too.'

You can't stay too long on mountain peaks.

'I'd sure like to run down this hill!' cried Sue, tossing back her shining hair. 'I'd like to race to the gate and astonish the sentry.'

Jiro prudently felt in his pocket for coins. 'Let's split the difference. Race you to the Canteen and the cokes on me.'

He and Kim and Sue flew down the sloping white road and waited at the canteen door, laughing and breathless, for the reproachful plodding Tomi.

That day was the high point. After it came the inevitable letdown, when Sue brought home her application papers and spent the evening hunched over them at her desk.

The first questions she filled in with some enjoyment. 'It's funny,' she said to her father, who sat spare and erect on one of the scarlet bridge chairs, reading and talking by turns. 'I suppose most folks like being the center of the stage, even when the audience is nothing but a printed paper. That's why they don't get madder at all the questionnaires in this day and age. But listen, Dad: "To the best of your knowledge name the organizations to which your father belonged, and the papers and magazines to which he has subscribed or which he has regularly read." How shall I answer that one? Rotary; Japanese-American

Citizens' League; Cordova Baptist Church? All right. And *Reader's Digest* and *Time* and *Geographic* and *Sat-EvePost* and *Cordova Journal?* Dad, do I have to mention that Tokyo paper?'

Kim said, 'I'm ashamed of you, Sis.'

Father surveyed her over his glasses. 'Aside from considerations of truth, you may be sure the F.B.I. knows just who has been taking Japanese papers.'

Sue said, 'Well, that's that, then,' wrote in the name and turned the page. '"List all the addresses at which you have ever lived — past twenty years." That won't waste much ink: 145 Dean Road, Cordova; Valley Forge, Santa Anita; Amache.'

She lettered on down the page, and paused. 'Of course I wasn't registered with Japanese or Spanish Consul, Dad? That means I'm not one of these dual citizens. Have I ever sent any of my children to Japan? No, not yet.' More chuckling, lettering, page-turning, and finally, '"If employment is desired, but no definite offer has been received, list kinds of employment acceptable in order of preference."'

Sue nibbled her pen thoughtfully. 'I could clerk in a store, with all the experience I had in yours. Maybe I better put that first and then care of children — Santa Anita and here. And then' — she sighed — 'then housework. Good grief, I hope my boss would have patience.'

Father shifted impatiently. 'It was kind to insist on giving your scholarship to your friend,' he said, 'but was it wise? It seems unreasonable to burden yourself with work for which you are not trained, and perhaps even lose your chance for college. You know it is required that you be reasonably certain of supporting yourself for at least a semester; and the small profits from my business still go back into its indebtedness. This Tomi, too — she may be a good young girl, but has she one-half your ability, my daughter?'

Sue flushed. 'Tomi needs pushing,' she argued. 'I can just see her parents marrying her off to someone she does not even like. They'd let her go to college — on a scholarship — though. And college might make the difference.'

'I have kept from saying it,' her father went on coldly, 'but the Oharas have done enough for the Itos.'

'You don't mean our sticking up for Jiro and Tomi against the gang?' Kim protested. 'Anyone would have done that.'

Mr. Ohara shook his head. 'Farther back. When Fuji Ito came to this country, long ago. My father had been a neighbor of his in Japan — mine of samurai stock, he a tradesman. And very poor. So I lent Fuji a substantial sum. And the amount I have received in repayment ——' he shrugged. 'Since the one time, years ago, when I sent for him to come to our house, there has been no mention of the debt between us. His excuses finished him for me.'

'Yet the Japanese have a reputation for paying their debts,' Kim remonstrated.

'Perhaps they think it is all in the family, when it is another Japanese who is the creditor.'

'Probably he's never had the money,' Sue stammered, hoping she did not look so uncomfortable as she felt. 'You know how shabby their house was, and their clothes. Maybe he thought of you as being well-fixed — not needing the money ——'

Mr. Ohara was regarding his daughter with a half-smile, but he did not look pleased. She hurried on:

'Jiro surely doesn't know this. Jiro'd never ——'

'It is not your place to defend the Ito family,' Father said sharply. 'You have no duties to the Itos.' He grated his chair back on the bricks and went out.

'Take the joy out of life, Sis?' Kim asked. 'I've been getting some knocks, too. Taro and his gang waylaid me last night and asked if I was volunteering. I thought I was in for a beating, six against one. But they only called me a traitor and a sucker and pushed me around a bit.'

'On the other hand, Kim, the real Americans in camp are getting up farewell feasts for you volunteers.'

'And on the other hand, Sis, Jiro's mother is treating him like a stranger.'

When Sue had finished her long questionnaire, that night, she relieved her heaviness with a letter to Emily:

Oh, Emily, you can't know what it's like to be thirsty with every pore for the only home you ever knew. I'm learning to like this climate, with its sort of exciting brilliance. And they say we have no idea of the beauty of the mountains, west and north of here; any more than Death Valley has any idea of California. But all the same, I'm famished for the sea. Some mornings I wake up and look at the sky and think, this is the right kind of sky for good swimming weather; and I can feel the waves lifting me and smell the salt water and hear the breakers and the sea-gulls. And then I remember.

And I'm famished for plain greenness and dampness. I'd like to stretch my body on wet, green grass, and crawl in under wet, green, blossoming bushes. And hear scads of mockingbirds singing and scolding.

She started a new page: *And, Emily, where am I going? Will folks draw away from me as if I had a disease? And shall we ever have college commencement together, as we vowed? Shall I ever get to college at all?*

That sheet she crumpled and dropped in the wastebasket. It might make Emily feel that they were disappointed in the business and the way Marian was handling it. She wrote instead: *Father thinks Marian and her*

*partner are marvelous to carry on the nursery and shop as
they have. We can never in this world repay you.*

Two days later, after the camp lights were on and evening mess was over, Mr. Ito called on the Oharas. He seated himself cautiously, settling into his chair as his thin, corded neck settled into his collar, without comfort. He giggled appreciatively at everything Father said, though often in the wrong places. Finally he came to the point.

'Your young people have been good friends to mine.'

Mr. Ohara's bow was stiff.

'But for your Sumi to give our Tomi her scholarship ——' Mr. Ito shook a wondering head.

Father murmured something cool and unintelligible.

'Tomiko, she cannot push herself out. And her mother wishes to engage go-betweens and make a marriage for the girl. But she would be willing that Tomi have college first.'

Father said, 'So our daughter has thought.'

'You think Sumi will do very well without the scholarship?' Mr. Ito asked hopefully. 'So able a young lady ——'

Mr. Ohara said, 'It is a fine day. For February.'

Mr. Ito sucked in his breath resignedly. 'It is not needful that your girl give up the scholarship,' he said. 'I —— By great care I can find the money for Tomi's college.'

Silence. Mrs. Ohara rose and noiselessly adjusted the red-appliquéd muslin curtains. Sue knew what her father must be thinking, and undoubtedly Mr. Ito knew. Slowly he drew from his pocket a worn billfold. Slowly he opened it and extracted a slip of pink paper.

'Doubtless you forget,' he said, staring fondly at the pink rectangle, 'that there was a small matter of a loan between us. It slipped from your mind, you with your money coming in large streams ——'

Father refused him the comfort of a nod.

'But I did not forget,' Mr. Ito went on reluctantly. 'Always we pinched and scraped; always we put aside every spare cent. Some day, I thought, when my savings grow big, I pay my honored friend the whole sum, not in wretched driblets. But——'

Every mind in the room must be focused on that pink paper. Mr. Ito blinked at it.

'The money in the bank has not grown big, and now it never will. But this I can pay on what I owe. For I consider that I owe it, even under these changed conditions.' Breathing hard, he slid the check across the table to Father.

Sue's keen eyes saw the figures penned on the paper. 'I shan't have to slow up my college work,' her spirit sang. 'I can give it all I've got.'

Mother asked, 'Will you have a cup of tea, Mr. Ito?'

Mr. Ito replied, 'Thank you, I must go home now,' and escaped, his face faintly shiny with sweat.

The Oharas were quiet till their caller had had time to get clear of the block. Then a ripple of laughter shook them. Perhaps it held more than a trace of hysteria; yet any laughter seemed good, it had been so long since Mother had even smiled.

'But this is — sort of mean,' Kim objected.

'Mean? He squeezed that check till it dripped — dripped his heart's blood,' said Father.

Sue knelt at his side. 'Dad,' she begged, 'can't we be friends with Tomi now? And Jiro?'

'Fuji is still a penny-pinching old boochie,' Father declared, picking up the check and crackling it fiercely. 'Not half what he owes me! Oh, well, it must be that Jiro takes back to his grandfather. I guess you could do worse.'

After that it was hurry, hurry, hurry! The spring semester was already well begun. Telegrams, Letters. Arrangements concluded for Sue and Tomi at the University of Denver. Choyo wistfully helping them and planning for her own expected relocation in the fall.

February, 1943, was a mild and gentle month in Colorado. The day before the girls' departure, Mitsu Ito's school class had gone down to the river and there had found violets blooming. She made a tight purple nosegay, backed with green leaves and a paper-lace doily, and brought it to Sue. When she dressed to go, Sue fastened it to the lapel of her suit, pinned it with the little pine Seabiscuit.

The Oharas and the Itos, Choyo and Shig, had got leave to see the girls off at Granada, and they stood waiting together for the train, which was late, as trains were expected to be in 1943. The townspeople had grown used to Japanese in these five months, and glanced at them only casually.

'To Denver takes only from now till the middle of the afternoon,' said Sue, her voice uneven with excitement. 'You must all come to see us.'

'When a fellow's inducted,' Jiro responded, 'he gets a little time to put his affairs in order. Then I'll come. And put my affairs in order,' he added under his breath.

Sue said, 'Everything begins to feel different, as soon as you get out of the barbed wire on "indefinite leave."'

'Everything?' Jiro asked.

'Everything,' Sue said huskily. She looked at her father and mother and Kim. She looked at Jiro. She saw no one beyond those four, though she smiled automatically at Shig and Choyo; though she stroked Kiku's shiny head and Mitsu was hanging on her arm. She wished the train would hurry. It was hard to leave those four to go back inside the barbed wire, so hard that she wanted to get it over with.

And then the whistle hooted far down the track, and she wished that the train would never come. 'You can't even get on with us,' she quavered. 'It's so late it'll hardly stop at all.'

Jiro had two-thirds of the bags, and he leaped up the steps after the girls, Kim following with the other luggage. Kim squeezed Sue's hand and grinned at Tomi, but Jiro only waited. 'Do me a favor and take Tomi in and find seats,' he said to Kim, and Kim, with an astonished grimace, obeyed.

Drawing Sue on into the entry, Jiro bent and kissed her on the mouth. She pressed her hand over the kiss he had left and stared up at him.

'Did it feel like one of Kim's?' he asked.

'I — don't think so,' she said. 'But when you come to Denver' — she breathed fast — 'then maybe we could try once more and make sure.'

Jiro did not wait for Denver. He kissed her again, joyously, and swung off the train after Kim, whose eyes were rolling wildly at what he had seen.

Sue moved into the vestibule and looked with bright, warm eyes at the group outside. 'It wasn't a bit like a brother, Jiro,' Sue told herself. 'And the years will pass, the years that hold us apart.'

The train jerked, and she grabbed a hand-rail for support, not taking her eyes from the people on the platform, her small parents, lean Kim, Shig, and Choyo, and the minister's family, hurrying up all out of breath. And Jiro.

She did not even notice the woman who held her dress aside and stared coldly as she crowded past Sue into the car. For there were the minister's family. And Jiro.

'Allll aboarrrd!' The call snapped triumphantly upward.

And now, O world, world! give us just a little chance!
Let us be human. Let us prove that we are Americans.

The train jerked, buckled, began to move, gathering
speed.

All aboard — and bound for America!

THE END